FAERY TALES

✦ FABER CLASSICS ✦

FAERY TALES

Carol Ann Duffy

FABER & FABER

With love and thanks to Melly Still and Tim Supple

This collection first published 2014
by Faber & Faber Limited
Bloomsbury House
74–77 Great Russell Street
London WC1B 3DA
This paperback edition first published in 2019

Collected Grimm Tales © Carol Ann Duffy, 1996, 1997, 2003
Beasts and Beauties © Carol Ann Duffy, 2004
Rats' Tales © Carol Ann Duffy, 2012
Illustrations © Tomislav Tomic, 2014

Typeset by Faber & Faber
Printed in the UK by CPI Group (UK) Ltd, Croydon CR0 4YY

A CIP record for this book
is available from the British Library

ISBN 978–0–571–36126–7

FSC
www.fsc.org
MIX
Paper from
responsible sources
FSC® C020471

2 4 6 8 10 9 7 5 3 1

For Ella, Matthew, Morgan and Nina –
beautiful children

Contents

Blue Beard

nce upon a time, there lived a man who owned many splendid properties in the town and in the country, who possessed an abundance of silver and gold plate, handcrafted furniture, the finest porcelain and glass, and coaches studded all over with sapphires. But he was the owner of something else as well – a blue beard which made him so appallingly ugly that women and girls took one look at him and fled.

He had a neighbour, a society lady, who had two fine sons and two daughters who were flowers of beauty. He asked her for one of the girls' hand in marriage and told her she could choose herself which one of them she would give to him as bride. Neither of the girls would have him, though, and they sent him backwards and forwards, up, down and sideways from one to the other, both adamant they would not marry a man with a blue beard. But there was one thing which repelled them even more and filled them with fear and revulsion. He had already been married to several wives and no one living knew what had happened to them.

Blue Beard, to try and win the girls over, escorted them with my lady, their mama, and three or four other mademoiselles of quality, and some fine young people of the district, to one of his country estates, where they were entertained for eight sumptuous days. So now it was all parties and candles and music and masks; it was hunting and shooting and fishing; it was dancing and feasting and the finest champagne and armagnac. It was *merci, monsieur* and *enchanté*, and *oooh la la*! In fact, everything went so splendidly, that the youngest daughter started to think that the lord of the manor's beard wasn't actually *bleu, mais non*, not really, and that he was a most civilised gentleman.

No sooner were they home than the marriage was held. A month after that, Blue Beard told his wife that he had to travel to a distant country for at least six weeks, on a matter of extreme importance. He encouraged her to amuse herself while he was away. She was to send for her friends and family, go to the countryside if she wished, and generally have a good time wherever she went. 'Here,' he said, 'are the keys to the two Great Rooms that contain my best and most costly furniture; these grant access to my silver and gold plate, which is to be used sparingly; these open my strong chests, which hold all my money; these my casket of jewels; and this here is the master key that opens all my apartments. But this little one here is the key to the closet at the far end of the great gallery. Open everything and go anywhere, but do not unlock the little closet. I forbid you this – and I want you to know that I forbid you this as night forbids day. If you disobey, there will be no hiding place here from my anger.' She promised to do everything just as he said and so he squeezed her to him, sandpapering her soft cheek with his blue beard, then climbed into his coach and began his journey.

Her friends and family didn't wait to be invited – they were so impatient to see all the splendour of the newlyweds' house. Only her brothers didn't come because their military duties delayed them. But all the others rushed straight to the two great rooms, flinging wide all the closets and wardrobes to gape and coo at the finery, which got more splendid with every door they opened. They could not say enough about their envy and delight at their friend's good fortune. She, however, paid not the slightest attention to all the treasures, because she was burning up with curiosity about the little closet. She became so consumed by this, that without even thinking how rude it was to abandon her guests, she rushed down the back stairs so recklessly that she could have broken her slender neck three times over.

When she reached the closet door, she hesitated for quite a while, remembering her husband's warnings, and worrying about the consequences if she disobeyed him. But temptation was far too strong for her and she could not resist it. She picked out the little key and opened the door, shaking all over. At first, she could make out nothing clearly at all, because the shutters were all closed. But after a few moments she saw that the floor was spattered with lumps of congealed blood, and upon it lay the bodies of several dead women, each sprawled there, or hanging in her wedding gown. These were the brides that Blue Beard had married and had slaughtered one after another. She nearly died of terror and as she jerked the key from the lock it fell from her hand. She tried to calm herself, picked up the key, locked the door, and hurried up the stairs to her chamber to try to recover. But she was too frightened. Then she noticed that the key to the closet was stained with blood, so she tried three times to scrub it off, but the blood would not come off even though she scoured it with soap and sand. The key was magic, and when she rubbed the blood from one side it would appear again on the other. That evening, when her guests said their *au revoirs*, she begged her sister to remain.

Unexpectedly, Blue Beard interrupted his journey and came home, saying that he had received a message on the road that the important business he was on his way to deal with was completed to his satisfaction. His wife did everything to act as though she was delighted by his sudden return. The next morning he asked her for the keys, but her hand shook so violently as she gave them to him that he guessed at once what had happened. 'Why is it,' he said, 'that the key to the closet is missing?' 'Oh! I must have left it upstairs on the table,' she said. 'Make sure,' said Blue Beard, 'that you fetch it to me quickly,' and after going backwards and forwards several times, she was forced to bring him the key. Blue Beard turned the key over and over, looking at it very carefully, then said to his wife, 'How did this blood get on the key?' 'I don't know,' answered the poor girl, white as a dead bride. 'You don't know,' said Blue Beard, 'you don't know, but *I* know. You were determined to go into the closet, weren't you? Very well, madame, you shall go in and take your place among the sisterhood you found there.'

At this, she flung herself at her husband's feet and

pleaded pitifully for his forgiveness, swearing that she was sorry and would never disobey him again. Even a stone would have been moved by her beauty and grief, but Blue Beard's heart was harder than any stone. 'You must die, *chérie*,' he said, 'and soon.' 'If I have to die,' she said through her tears, 'then allow me a little time to dress in my bridal shroud.' 'You can have a quarter of an hour,' said Blue Beard, 'but not a second longer.'

As soon as she was alone, she called to her sister and said, 'Sister, I need you to climb up to the top of the tower and see if my brothers are coming. They promised me they would come here today, so if you see them then give them a signal to hurry.' Her sister went up to the top of the tower, and the terrified woman cried out, 'Sister, Sister, do you see anything coming?' And her sister replied, 'I see nothing but the sun making dust and the grass growing green.' Meanwhile, Blue Beard was sharpening and sharpening a huge knife, and chanting horribly:

Sharper, sharper, shiny knife,
Cut the throat of whiny wife!

Then he shouted out, 'Come down at once or I'll come up to you!' 'Just one moment longer, please,' said his wife, 'first I have to fasten my bodice and pull on my silken stockings;' and then she called up very softly, 'Sister, Sister, do you see anything coming?' And her sister said, 'I see nothing but the sun and the dust and the grass.' Blue Beard was sharpening and chanting even more ferociously:

Sharper, sharper, knife so dear,
Slit her throat from ear to ear!

'Get down here now!' he bawled, 'or I'll come up to you.' 'I'm coming,' said his wife, 'I just have to tie my garter and slip on my shoes,' and then she cried out, 'Sister, Sister, do you see anything coming?' 'I see,' answered her sister, 'a great dust rolling in on this side here.' 'Is it my brothers?' 'Oh no, my dear sister! It's just a flock of sheep.' Blue Beard sharpened and chanted even more vigorously:

Now the knife is sharp enough,
And ready for the bloody stuff!

'Come down here now!' he bellowed, 'or I'll be up for you!' 'One last moment,' said his wife, 'I have only my veil to secure and my white kid gloves.' Then she cried, 'Sister, Sister, do you see anything coming?' 'I can see,' she said, 'two horsemen coming, but they are still a long way off. Thanks be to God,' she cried at once, 'it is our brothers! I have made them a sign to gallop.' Blue Beard roared out now so loudly that the whole house shook.

The poor woman came down and collapsed at his feet, with her face jewelled with tears and her hair loose about her shoulders. 'This won't help,' said Blue Beard, 'you must die;' then, grasping her hair with one hand and raising the cutlass with the other, he was about to cut off her head. His wife writhed around and, looking at him with dying eyes, begged him for one last moment to calm herself. 'No, no, no,' he said, 'give yourself over to God!' At this precise moment there came such a thunderous knocking at the gates that Blue Beard froze. The gates were opened and immediately the two horsemen entered. They saw Blue Beard, drew their swords and rushed straight at him. Blue Beard recognised that they were the brothers of his wife – one a dragoon and the other a musketeer – so he ran for his life. But the brothers were too fast for him and caught him before he even reached the steps to the porch. Then they skewered their swords through his body and left him there dead.

Their poor sister was scarcely more alive than her husband and was too weak to stand and embrace her brothers. Blue Beard had no heirs and so his wife became owner of all his estate. With one part, she gave a dowry to her sister, to marry a young gentleman who had loved her truly for a long time; another part she spent to buy captains' commissions for her brothers, and she used the rest to marry herself to a very kind, clean-shaven gentleman, who soon made her forget the dark time she had spent with Blue Beard.

The Husband Who Was to Mind the House for the Day

man once stomped about northern parts who was so grumpy and surly that he thought his wife could do nowt right in the house. So one evening, during harvest time, he came cursing, blowing and fuming home, showing his teeth and kicking up a right dust.

'My love, you mustn't be so angry,' said his goody. 'Tomorrow why don't we swap our work? I'll go out with the mowers and mow, and you can keep house at home.'

Aye, the husband thought, that would do nicely. He was agreeable to that, he said.

So, first thing next morning, his goody put the scythe over her neck and walked out into the hayfield with the mowers and set off mowing. And the man was to stop at home, mind the house, and do the housework.

His first task was to churn the butter, but when he had churned for a bit, he worked up a thirst, and went down to the cellar to tap a barrel of ale. But just when he had knocked in the bung and was fitting the tap to the cask, above his head he heard the pig lumber into the kitchen. So off he legged it up the cellar steps, the tap in his fist, as fast as he could, to sort out the pig before it knocked over the churn. But the pig had already knocked over the churn, and stood there, snuffling and rooting in the cream, which was pouring all over the floor. The husband became so mad with rage that he forgot about the ale barrel and charged at the pig as hard as he could. He caught it as well, just as it squealed through the door, and landed it such a kick that poor piggy lay for dead on the ground. Then he remembered he had the tap in his hand; but when he ran down to the cellar, every last drop of ale had dripped out of the cask.

So he went into the dairy and found enough leftover cream to fill the churn again, and he started up churning once more, for there'd better be butter at dinner. After he'd churned for a while, he remembered that their milking cow was still locked up in the cowshed and hadn't been fed or watered all morning, even though the sun was riding high in the sky. But then he thought it was too far to lead her down to the meadow, so he'd just put her up on the top of the house. The house, you should realise, had a roof which was thatched with sods and a thick crop of grass had sprouted up there. The house was built close to a steep slope and he reckoned that if he laid a plank across to the thatch at the back, he'd get the cow up no problem.

But he still couldn't leave the churn because there was his baby crawling around on the floor and, 'If I leave it,' he thought, 'the child is sure to knock it over.' So he heaved the churn onto his back and went off out; but then he thought he'd best water the cow before he put her up on the thatch; so he picked up a bucket to draw water from the well but, as he bent over the mouth of the well, all the cream poured out of the churn over his shoulders and vanished into the well. Then he gave the cow some water and put her up on the thatch.

It was getting near dinnertime and he hadn't

even sorted the butter yet, so he decided he'd better
boil up the porridge, so he filled the pot with water
and hung it over the fire. When he'd done that, he
worried that the cow might fall off the roof and break
her neck or her legs, so he climbed onto the roof to tie
her up. He tied one end of the rope round the cow's
neck and made it safe, and the other
end he slid down the chimney and tied
it round his own thigh. And he had
to get a move on, because the water
was bubbling in the pot and he
hadn't even begun grinding
the oatmeal yet.

So he started to grind away; but while he was going at it hammer and tongs, the cow fell off the top of the house anyway, and as she fell, she dragged the man up the chimney by his leg. He was stuck there like a cork in a bottle and the cow hung halfway down the wall, dangling between heaven and earth, unable to get either up or down.

Meanwhile, the goody had been waiting seven lengths and seven widths of the field for her husband to call her to dinner, but no call came. Finally, she reckoned she'd worked and waited long enough, so she went home. The moment she got there she saw the tragic sight of the cow swinging on the wall, so she ran up and cut the rope in two with her scythe. As soon as she did this, her husband came crashing down out of the chimney, and so, when his missus came into the kitchen, there she found her baby cradling the half-dead pig and her husband standing on his brainbox in the porridge pot. This is what happened the day the husband was to mind the house.

No surprise there then, eh?

15

The Three Wishes

It was a very long time ago, and it was once, that a poor woodman dwelled in a great English forest. Every day that he lived, out he went to fell timber. One fine day, off he went and the wood-wife packed his pouch and looped his bottle over his shoulder and under his oxter, and that was his meat and drink for the forest. He had his eye on a huge old oak, reckoning it would yield strong planks aplenty. When he stood beneath it, out came his axe and around his bonce it swung as though he was trying to deck the oak with a stroke. But he hadn't landed so much as a blow when his ears heard pitiful plaintive pleas and he clapped eyes on a fairy, who begged and beseeched him to spare the tree. He was stunned – you can imagine – with fascination and fear, and he couldn't force one word through his lips. At last he found his tongue. 'Well,' he said, 'I'll do as thou wants.'

'You have done yourself a greater favour than you know,' replied the fairy, 'and I propose to show my gratitude by granting you your next three wishes, whatever they may be.' At that, the fairy was nowhere to be seen and the woodman hung his pouch over his shoulder and slung his bottle at his side and loped for home.

Well, the way was a long one and the poor man was flummoxed and flabbergasted by the magical thing that had happened to him, and when he got home there was nowt in his noddle but a strong desire to sit in his chair and rest. Perhaps this was the work of the fairy? Your guess. Anyroad, he plonked himself down next to the toasty fire and as he sat he grew hungry, even though it was a long time till supper.

'Has thou owt for supper, wife?' he called to the wood-wife.

'Nowt for a couple of hours yet,' she said.

'Aah!' groaned the woodman. 'I wish I had a long strong link of black pudding in front of my face!'

No sooner had the words left his lips when bonk,

slither, clatter and clunk, what should fall down the chimney but a long strong link of the finest black pudding a man's belly could desire.

If the woodman gaped, the wood-wife gawped to the power of three. 'What's happened here?' she said.

Then the woodman remembered the morning's events and he told his story from start to finish, and as he told it the wood-wife glowered and glared, and when he'd finished she exploded, 'Thou fool! Thou fool! Thou fool! I wish the pudding was on your nose, I really do!'

And before you could say Flingo Macbingo, there the good man sat and his neb was longer by a noble length of black pudding.

He gave a tug, but it stuck, and she gave a yank, but it stuck, then they both pulled till they nearly tore off his conk, but it stuck and it stuck and it stuck.

'What's to happen now?' he said.

'It doesn't look that bad,' she said, giving him a good looking over.

Then the woodman realised that he must wish and wish quick; so wish he did and his wish was for the black pudding to be off his nose. Alleluia! There it gleamed in a dish on the table, and if the woodman and wood-wife never rode in a fairy-tale coach or danced in satin and silk, well, at least they had as splendid a link of long strong black pudding as ever the heart and stomach of a man or his missus could wish for.

Beauty and the Beast

nce upon a time, there was a rich merchant who had three daughters. The girls were just as clever as they were *bella* and none more so than the youngest, whose name was Beauty. Her sisters were jealous of her. They swanned about going to parties and pageants and jeered at Beauty because she liked to stay at home with her books. Many suitors came to court the three girls. The two eldest trilled that they would consider betrothal to nothing below a count, so there! Beauty, in her turn, gently thanked the eligible young men but chose to remain in her father's house for a while yet.

One dark day, the merchant lost all his fortune. Only the tears in his eyes were silver as he told his daughters that his wealth was gone. They must all move at once to the country and work for their living. This was a dreadful shock to the girls, who had never lifted a dainty finger in their lives. Beauty got up at first light to cook, clean, make, mend, tidy, scour and scrub. But she made sure she read her books too, and in less than a couple of months she was fitter and bonnier than ever. Her two sisters, however, did nothing but whine and whinge about the loss of their fine frocks and fancy friends. 'And look at her,' they moaned one to the other, 'how snide she is to be happy with such an awful life!' But Beauty's father was proud of his hard-working, modest daughter.

A grim year passed, then one morning the merchant received news of the safe arrival of one of his ships that had been thought lost. The two eldest girls were in raptures and demanded a wardrobe of expensive dresses so they could shimmy back to society in high style. Beauty privately thought that their father's money would hardly stretch to one gown each, but rather than seem to be critical of her sisters' eager pestering she asked for a rose.

The Merchant set off to reclaim his cargo, but

there were debts to be paid and legal matters to settle and, after a bundle of trouble, he had to head for home as penniless as before. As he returned through the Great Forest, a blinding snowstorm, like a frenzy of torn-up paper money, raged around him and he lost his way. It was foolhardy to struggle on through the icy blizzard, but he knew if he stayed put he would freeze to death and already he could hear the bloodthirsty howling of wolves who had sniffed him out. Exhausted and on the lip of despair, he saw – thank God! – a light in the distance and ran, ran for his life, until he reached a magnificent castle.

The doors were open. In he went to make himself known but there was no reply to his hellos. Only the fire spat and crackled and he saw that the table was sumptuously laid for one. 'I hope the master here or his servants will forgive this intrusion!' He waited and waited until it looked like all the good food and wine would be wasted, so he sat down nervously and began to eat and drink. He ate with jittery gusto and after a glass of vino or four he plucked up the courage to explore the castle. He came to a room with the softest, plumpest of beds in it. He lay down, tired to his bones, and fell fast asleep.

It was late next morning when he was awakened by the rich scent of hot chocolate and sweet biscotti. He sniffed gratefully! 'This castle must belong to a kind spirit who has taken pity on me! *Grazzi*, dear good spirit!' Outside, instead of snow, was the most beautiful rose garden anyone with eyes under his eyebrows had ever seen. Remembering Beauty's request, he stepped outside to pick her a rose. The sweet, heady perfume of an opening red rose drew him towards it, but as he snapped its stem he was nearly deafened by the horrifying roar of some kind of beast charging at him.

'Ungrateful man!' thundered the creature. 'I have saved your life by letting you into my castle and to thank me you steal one of my roses, which I prize over everything! You have one quarter of an hour before you meet death!'

The merchant fell to his knees and raised up his hands.

'My Lord, I beg you to pardon me! Believe me, I didn't know I would offend you by picking a rose for my youngest daughter!'

'My name is not My Lord,' snarled the beast.

'Don't flatter me. My name is Beast. You say you have daughters. I will spare your life on one condition – that one of them comes here of her own free will and suffers for your sake. Swear that if none of your daughters offers to die in your place you will return here within three months.'

The merchant had no intention of sacrificing one of his girls, but he thought that by agreeing to the bargain he could at least say a proper goodbye to them. He swore on oath to return and then he left the castle with as much despair as he had entered it with relief.

By the time the moon was up, the good man was home. His daughters ran to meet him but instead of hugging them happily, he held out the rose and wept.

'Take it, Beauty,' he sobbed, 'though you cannot imagine the price I must pay for it.'

Then he told them his terrible tale. At once, her elder sisters rounded on Beauty viciously. So much for her pride! She couldn't just ask for pretty dresses like they did. Oh no! Miss Goody Two-Shoes had to *distinguish* her stuck-up saintly self and now she would be the *death* of their poor father. And look at her! Completely dry-eyed! How *callous*! How *heartless*!

'Why should I shed any tears?' said Beauty. 'If the monster will take any one of us three then I will volunteer to quench his fury. Earning my father his life will prove my love for him.'

'Don't even think of it,' cried the merchant. 'I am old and my life is nearly done. I cannot accept this precious gift.'

But Beauty would not be dissuaded and he had to agree. Her two sisters were well pleased because Beauty's goodness drove them crazy and they were glad to be shot of her. And when the day came for Beauty to leave, they had to scrub at each other's hard eyes with an onion to squeeze out a few tears.

The merchant and his youngest child journeyed to the castle and discovered in the great hall there a table plentifully laid for two. 'The Beast wants to fatten me up before he devours me,' thought Beauty. At last the Beast stood before them and Beauty recoiled at his sickening appearance, but promised she had come of her own free will.

'You are good,' said the Beast, 'and I appreciate this, honest man. Get on your way now and take this chest of gold to buy costly silks for your other daughters. Don't ever think of returning here.'

The Beast vanished as suddenly as he'd appeared.

'Oh, Beauty,' croaked the merchant, 'I am scared half out of my wits for you. Let me be the one to stay!'

'No,' said Beauty firmly and to comfort her father she smiled warmly and hugged him. But the wretched man cried bitterly when he left his beloved child.

Now the poor girl was all alone for her last few hours. She wandered through the fine castle, noticing every charming thing. Before long she came to a door above which was written her own name. Inside was a wonderful collection of books that made her gasp with pleasure. Her eye fell on a book of gold. Inside was written:

Welcome, Beauty. Have no fear.
You are Queen and govern here.
Say your heart's desires aloud,
Your secret wishes. Don't be proud.

'My only wish is to see my father.'

No sooner had the words left her lips than she noticed a mirror and was amazed to see within it her father arriving home, safe but almost broken with grief. Her sisters were pretending to share his sorrow but they could barely keep the satisfaction of getting rid of Beauty off their faces. A moment later the image faded and was gone.

That night Beauty was treated to a splendid musical concert, but she didn't see a soul. Despite everything, she felt strangely at peace and drifted out into the garden to luxuriate in the perfumes of her favourite flowers. A gross and hideous noise made her jump and she couldn't stop herself exclaiming with shock as she found herself staring straight into the hot, ravenous eyes of Beast. Blood dripped from his teeth and in his jaws was the raw flesh of a freshly killed animal. Beauty froze. Beast's naked shape cringed in unspeakable shame and a heartstopping wail filled the night as he fled.

Beauty could not remember how she had got to her bedchamber that night. When she awoke in the morning she thought the whole frightful incident had been a nightmare. But there was a note on her pillow which read: 'From now on you shall walk in the gardens undisturbed.'

The next night at supper, to Beauty's horror, Beast was there, dressed in his best velvet *capa*. He was courteous and polite and Beauty noticed that he tried his best to display excellent table manners. But the noises he made when he ate disgusted her and she couldn't hide this. Beast hung his head and said:

'Forgive me, Beauty.'

She could tell he meant it and she swallowed hard and nodded. But Beast saw that she hadn't touched her food and said: 'If my presence distresses you, I will leave at once. Do I revolt you?'

'I cannot lie. You do. But I know you are very . . . good-natured.'

'Yes. Even so, I am a monster.'

'There are plenty who deserve that name more than you do. I prefer you to someone who conceals a twisted heart behind an upright form.'

'I am grateful to you.' After a pause the Beast continued, 'Beauty? Will you consent to be my wife?'

Beauty gagged at these words and it was some time before she summoned the nerve to answer him. But at last she said shaking, 'No, Beast.'

The poor monster hissed dreadfully, like a thousand snakes, and the whole castle echoed. He withdrew at once, leaving Beauty to suffer a tangled knot of revulsion and compassion.

Time passed. Compassion grew like a rose and the weed of revulsion withered. Beauty had spent three contented months in the castle. Each evening Beast came to her and they were good companions, talking, reading or listening to music. She had grown used to his grotesque features and eating problems and instead of dreading his visits would find herself looking at the clock to check when he was coming. Only one thing troubled her. Every night before she retired, the monster asked if she would be his wife. One evening she said to him:

'Beast, your question makes me anxious. I wish I could agree to marry you, but I can't. I shall always be fond of you as a friend. Please try to be happy with that.'

'I ought to be happy as we are, because I know how badly I'm afflicted. I value friendship, too, but I love you, Beauty, deeply and tenderly. Promise me this: you will never leave me.'

Beauty coloured and answered truthfully that she

promised never to leave him. Then she added: 'But if I don't see my father again, I shall *never* be happy.'

'I would rather die than make you unhappy.'

'I swear to you that I will return in one week.'

'Then you shall be there in the morning,' said Beast. 'When you want to come back to me, lay this ring on a table before you fall asleep. *Arrivederci*, Beauty.'

When she awoke the next day, Beauty was in her father's house, which was still out in the country despite the gold that Beast had given. The good man thought he would die of shock and happiness when he saw his treasured Beauty again. He summoned her two sisters, who had moved to town with their new husbands. They were both deeply unhappy. The eldest had married a gorgeous gentleman, but he fancied himself so much he never looked at her. The second had wed a man famed for his wit, but he only used it now to torment and torture his wife.

Beauty's sisters nearly fell down with envy when they saw her dressed as a princess and glowing radiantly.

'Sister,' seethed the eldest, 'I have an idea. Let's try to keep Miss Perfect here for more than a week and, who knows, the stupid monster will be so angry she didn't keep her promise that he'll eat her.'

'Excellent,' agreed the other. 'We must show her as much kindness as we can.'

They managed this so well that their younger sister was truly touched and when the week was over she was easily won over by their tears and entreaties.

So the family enjoyed more precious days together, but as each one passed Beauty felt more and more anxious about deserting Beast. It wasn't just that she'd broken her promise – she longed to see him again. She caught herself thinking about his kind heart and his thoughtfulness. She remembered the desolate look in his eyes when she turned down his offer of marriage. She was sorry he was so hideous, but she thought, 'It's not his fault. And I know I'd be much happier with him than my sisters are with their husbands. I might not love him in the way that he loves me, but we are good friends. I can't stand making him so unhappy.'

So she put her ring on the table and went to bed.

When she awoke the next morning she realised that she felt true joy at being back in Beast's castle. She dressed in her loveliest gown and counted the hours and minutes until evening. But the castle held only silence and there was no Beast. Fearful about his disappearance and distraught that she might be the cause of it, Beauty ran weeping and crying all through the castle. Beast was nowhere. She lit a torch and ran into the garden, desperately calling his name.

At last, she found him, motionless, cold, sodden, under a rose bush. Beauty flung herself upon him, afraid he was dead, and pressed her heart to his as her tears blessed his face. 'I thought I had lost you,' gasped Beast, 'but now I am seeing you for the last time, I can die happy.'

'No, Beast!' sobbed Beauty. 'My dear, dear Beast, please don't die. This terrible grief I feel tells me that I cannot live without you. I thought we could only be friends but now I know . . . I love you, Beast. *Ti voglio bene.*'

As Beauty uttered these words the whole castle burst into light and was filled with sweet music. Beauty stared in wonder but when she turned back to Beast he was gone. At her feet lay a man. Although he was handsome and well-made, she asked anxiously, 'Where is Beast?'

'You're looking at him,' he smiled. 'Let me explain. Because I was too proud and arrogant to properly rule my kingdom, I was cursed by a powerful spell to take the form of a beast. The spell could only be broken if an honest and true woman would willingly agree to marry me. There was only you in this whole wide world generous enough see my repentant heart and be won by it. I offer you my hand and with it my crown.'

Beauty, surprised and delighted, gave her hand to the charming Prince and together they returned to the castle. Her family had been taken there and she ran to her father's arms. But when she looked at her sisters, they turned into statues, paralysed by jealousy and condemned to stand before their sister's castle gates, watching and watching her happiness.

The Emperor's New Clothes

he people had an Emperor once, who was so terribly keen on fashion that he spent all his money on fine new clothes. He took absolutely no interest in his army, or going to the theatre, and would only drive through the country in order to show off his latest outfit. He had different clothes for every hour of the day, twenty-four seven, and just as we say of the King that he's in a meeting, it was always said of the Emperor, 'He's in his wardrobe.'

The Emperor lived in the capital city, a vibrant, exciting place. Every day saw new people pouring in, and one day two swindlers showed up. They put it about that they were weavers and could weave the finest garments anyone could imagine. Not only were their colours and designs incredibly attractive, but the clothes made from their material had the amazing quality of being invisible to anyone who wasn't fit for the position he held or who was well stupid.

'Gosh! They must be wonderful clothes,' thought the Emperor. 'If I wore them, I'd be able to tell which of my statesmen are unfit for their posts! And I'd be able to sort the clever ones from the thick. Yes! The stuff must be woven for me at once!' And he arranged for a large amount of cash to be paid to the swindlers, so that they could start work immediately.

So they did – they set up a couple of looms and pretended to be weaving away, but there was absolutely nothing in the looms. Nowt. Zilch. Cool as you like, they demanded the most delicate silk and the finest gold thread, which they promptly stashed in their own pockets; and then they went on weaving nothing far into the small hours at their empty looms.

'Gosh! I wonder how they're getting on with the stuff,' said the Emperor to himself. But there was one thing that was really worrying him – and this was that a man who was stupid or quite unfit for his position would never be able to see what had been woven. Not that he had anything to fear on his own account, not at all, not at all, but, all the same, it was probably sensible to send along somebody else first to see how things were coming along. The whole city had heard of the strange power possessed by the material and everyone was desperate to find out how crap or daft their neighbours were.

'I'll send my honest Prime Minister to the weavers,' thought the Emperor. 'He's the best one to tell what the cloth looks like, for he has brains and no one deserves his position more than him.'

So off went the honest Prime Minister to the workshop where the two swindlers sat cheating at their empty looms.

'Good heavens above!' thought the Prime Minister, with his eyes frogging out of his head. 'I can't see anything at all!' But he made sure not to say so.

The two swindlers begged him to come nearer and take a closer look. Didn't he think their colours and patterns were wonderful? Then they pointed to their empty looms and although the poor Prime Minister widened and widened his eyes, he couldn't see a thing because there wasn't a thing to see. 'Crikey!' he thought. 'Does this mean that I am stupid? I had no idea! Nobody else had better get wind of it either!

Am I unfit for my post? No, I can't possibly admit that I can't see the stuff.'

'What d'you think of it then?' asked one of the weavers.

'Oh, it's so charming! Quite enchanting! Totally exquisite!' said the poor Prime Minister, staring through his spectacles. 'What an original pattern! What tasteful colours! Yes, indeed, I shall make sure to tell the Emperor how much I like it!'

'Oh, we're well pleased to hear that,' said the swindlers, and then they named all the colours and described the unusual design. The Prime Minister listened carefully, so he could repeat it all to the Emperor – which he did.

Now the swindlers demanded more money, more fine silk and more gold thread, which they said was needed for weaving. But it all went straight into their own sky-rockets – not one thread went onto the loom – and they carried on working at the empty frames as before.

Before too long, the Emperor sent along another sincere statesman to see how the weaving was coming along and if the stuff would soon be ready. Just like the Prime Minister, he looked and looked, but, as there was nothing there, there was nothing to see.

'Look at that! Isn't that a well gorgeous piece of stuff?' said the swindlers, and they drew his attention to the prettiness of the design, which wasn't there at all.

'I know I'm not stupid,' thought the man, 'so it must be my official position I'm not fit for. Some people would have a good laugh at this, so I must make sure it doesn't get out.' So he praised the material, which he could not see, and complimented them on its beautiful colours and charming design. 'Yes, it's fabulous!' he said to the Emperor when he got back.

The whole town could talk of nothing else but the wonderful material. The Emperor decided that he himself must see it while it was still on the loom. With a crowd of hand-picked courtiers, including the two esteemed officials who had already visited, the Emperor arrived at the workshop. Both crafty villains were weaving away like the clappers without so much as a thread between them.

'Isn't it splendid, Your Imperial Majesty?' said the two honest statesmen. 'What colouring! What patterning! If Your Majesty will take a look!' And they pointed to the empty looms, quite sure that everyone else could see the stuff.

'Gosh! What's going on?' thought the Emperor. 'I can see nothing at all! This is dreadful! Am I stupid? Am I unfit to be Emperor? This is the most appalling thing that could happen to me . . . Oh, it's so-o-o gorgeous,' he said to them. 'It has our total approval!' And he nodded his head up and down contentedly as he gazed at the empty loom. After all, he wasn't going to say that he couldn't see a thing. The crowd of courtiers who had come with him looked and looked, but they could see no more than anyone else had done. But they all copied the Emperor and said, 'Oh, it's so-o-o gorgeous!' And then they advised him to have some clothes made from this wonderful new material and to wear them for the Grand Procession that was soon to take place. 'Beautiful!' 'Divine!' 'Superb!' 'To die for!' were the compliments that scurried from mouth to mouth. Everyone just *loved* the material and the Emperor gave each of the swindlers a knighthood, with a badge for his buttonhole, and the title of Imperial Weaver.

On the eve of the Grand Procession, the swindlers sat up all night by the light of seventeen candles. Everyone could see how hard they were working to finish the Emperor's new clothes. They pretended to take the material down from the loom; they snipped and they clipped at the air with huge scissors; they sewed busily with needles that had no thread in them, and at the end of it all they said, 'Sorted! The Emperor's new clothes are ready!'

Then the Emperor himself arrived, surrounded by all his statesmen; and the two swindlers held out their arms, as though they were displaying the new clothes, and said, 'Here are the trousers! Here is the jacket! Here is the long cloak!' And so on. 'They are as delicate as gossamer, as light as a spider's web; you can hardly feel you are wearing anything – that's the beauty of them!'

'Yes! Absolutely!' chorused all the statesmen. But they could see nothing, because nothing was there.

'Now, if Your Imperial Majesty will be gracious enough to take off your clothes,' said the swindlers, 'then we will dress you in the new clothes right here in front of this big mirror.'

So the Emperor took off all his clothes, and the swindlers pretended to hand him each of the new garments they were supposed to have made. Then they made out they were zipping up the trousers and straightening the collar and draping the cloak.

'Wonderful! It's amazing how well they suit Your Majesty! What a terrific fit!' everyone started to say. 'What a pattern! What colours! What a gorgeous cloak!'

The Master of Ceremonies entered with an announcement. 'The canopy to be borne above Your Majesty in the procession has arrived outside.'

'Very well, I am ready,' said the Emperor. 'Don't they suit me down to the ground?' And he posed again in front of the mirror, trying to look as though he was gazing at his splendid new clothes.

The servants, who were to carry the cloak, stooped down and groped about on the floor, as if they were picking up the cloak, and as they walked they pretended to be holding something up in the air, not daring to let on that they couldn't see anything.

So the Emperor marched under the canopy in the Grand Procession, and all the people in the streets and hanging out of the windows said, 'Look! The Emperor's new clothes are the finest he has ever had! What a perfect fit! What a gorgeous cloak!' No one would let anyone else know that he couldn't see anything, because that would have meant he was

unfit for his job or incredibly stupid. Never had the Emperor's clothes been such a howling success.

'But he's got nothing on!' shouted a little child.

'Good grief!' exclaimed the courtiers. 'Stupid child! His parents should take him home! It's ridiculous!' But the child's remark was whispered from one person to another.

'He's got nothing on! There's a little child saying he hasn't got anything on!'

'He hasn't got anything on!' shouted all the people at last. And the Emperor felt really uncomfortable, because it seemed to him that they were quite right. But somehow he thought to himself, 'Gosh, well, I must go through with it, procession and all.' So he drew himself proudly up to his full height, while his servants marched behind his behind, holding up the cloak that wasn't there.

Toby and the Wolf

young miller hereabouts had a dog called Toby, passed down from his father. The old hound was getting long in the tooth, and had grown hard of hearing, so he couldn't guard the house as well as he used to. The miller neglected Toby, and the servants behaved as their master did. They gave Toby some shoe-leather whenever they passed him, and as often as not forgot to feed him. Toby had such a grim time of it, that he made up his mind to turn his back on the mill and chance his luck in the woods. On the way, he bumped into a wolf, who greeted him, '*Nazdar!* Comrade Toby! Where are you heading?'

The dog told him what he had to put up with back

at the mill, and swore he would stick it no longer.

'Brother Toby,' said the wolf, 'you've got plenty of years, but precious little nous. Why leave the mill now, in your old age, and scrape a miserable existence in the woods? Twice, when you were young, you saved the mill from bandits, and now I'm hearing how disgracefully you've been treated! Take a tip from Wolfie, and go back to the mill and see to it that the miller feeds you properly.'

'Comrade Wolf,' said Toby, 'I would rather die of hunger than crawl back there.'

'Don't be so headstrong, Brother Toby,' said the wolf. 'Between us we'll find the answer to your problems! Now, tomorrow, when the nursemaid comes out to the field that the miller is harvesting, she'll be carrying his baby son. The moment she puts him down, I'll sneak up and make off with him. Your job is to sniff out my trail and follow it. I'll drop the brat in the grass beneath the great oak tree for you to find. Pick him up, take him back to the miller, and he'll greet you like a hero!'

The next day, the nursemaid went up to the field with food for the harvesters, and in one arm she was carrying the miller's baby son. When she reached the field, she laid the baby down on a sheaf and started up joking and flirting with the reapers. The wolf crept up, seized the infant, and sped away into the woods.

When the maid saw the wolf running for the trees with the baby in its jaws, she chased after it, sobbing and screaming for help, and too afraid to go home without her master's child. In the meantime, the harvesters had sent a lad sprinting back to the mill to tell the miller what had happened. Half out of his mind with distress, the miller rushed to fetch the hunter, and the pair of them legged it into the woods. But before they'd got very far, Toby appeared back at the mill, carrying the baby safely in his mouth. The miller's wife came running out, crying with joy, and she scooped up the baby and laid him in his cot. Then she patted and stroked Toby's head and ordered that bread and milk be set down before him at once.

When the miller came back and was told how Toby had saved his son, he felt so ashamed that he had neglected the old dog that he swore Toby would have nothing but the best from that day forward. And as the tale of the rescue spread, Toby was given a hero's welcome wherever he went.

One day, the wolf turned up to see Toby as he lay

in the sun at the back of the mill. 'Admit it, Brother, how sound my advice was,' began the wolf. 'You live in the lap of plenty now, so don't forget! One good turn deserves another! I haven't eaten for a week and I need you to help me.'

Toby nodded. Then he said, 'No problem, Brother Wolf. One of the maids is to be married tomorrow and the pantry is stuffed full of meat and pastry and other good scoff for the wedding feast. Let's wait till dark: then we can get into the pantry through the back window and have a feast all of our own!'

So that evening, when darkness fell, the two cronies climbed through the pantry window. They stuffed and supped all night until the wolf grew reckless. 'Brother Toby!' he yelled. 'I'm so happy, I feel like a good old singsong!'

'You'd better shut up and get out of here quickly,' warned Toby, 'or we'll both be discovered and beaten!'

But the wolf had lost the plot and threw back his head with a wild wolf howl, and his racket could be heard all over the house. The miller woke up and searched every room in the mill before he remembered that the food for the wedding banquet was laid out in the pantry. He went to look and found Toby and the wolf. He snatched up a stick and laid into the two thieves, beating them until the hair flew from their pelts.

The wolf finally managed to escape, but the miller collared Toby and chained him up. In the morning, the miller's wife pleaded with him to let Toby off the chain, insisting that he must have been led astray by the wolf. So the miller removed the chain but warned Toby to keep well clear of the wolf.

Time passed, and late one night the wolf crept into the mill to persuade Toby to take revenge on the miller for the beating. Toby pointed out that the miller owned a powerful shotgun and could easily shoot them dead. But the wolf wouldn't be put off, and bragged of his strength and cunning.

'Ach, Brother Toby,' sneered the wolf, 'you're talking like a coward. I'm not going to leave this place with an empty belly. The miller owns a fat old ram. For old times' sake, I want you to drive it out of the flock for me. That way, I can kill it easily and eat my fill without any bother.'

Toby remembered the miller's warning about the wolf. Toby enjoyed his life at the mill now, and he had no desire to chuck it all away. But when he saw how angry the wolf was becoming, he grew scared of him and said, 'Brother Wolf, the ram would be certain to bleat and the miller will come running. You must stand in front of the sheep pen with your mouth open. When I drive the ram out, you must seize him by the head to stop him bleating and drag him off to the woods sharpish.'

The wolf was all for this and took up position outside the sheep pen. Toby jumped inside and drove the big strong ram towards the eager wolf. But the ram butted the wolf's butt and the wolf turned a somersault and crashed down in the yard, unable to move. He moaned and groaned, and wheezed, 'Brother Toby, the ram has knocked the breath out of my body! Keep him away from me!'

The miller heard the wolf crying. He saw the ram out in the yard and the wolf there too. He snatched up his shotgun and fired at the wolf. But although he hit him in the rear, the wolf managed to drag himself away.

Toby stretched out in his kennel, well pleased at the way matters had turned out. He told himself that he would never listen to the wolf again. But a few days later, what happened but the wolf turned up again at the mill to see Toby. 'We have to make the miller suffer for shooting at me,' he said. 'I have three pellets lodged in my arse. To get even with him, I'm going to destroy his favourite colt.'

Toby pleaded with the wolf not to do this, and said he would have no part in such a revenge. But the wolf bared his fangs at Toby. 'I will pin you down and sink my teeth into your scrawny throat if you refuse to help me,' he snarled. 'Do what I say this instant or you won't move from here alive. Drive the colt out of the stable so that I can fall upon it.'

The yard was deserted and Toby knew that he could never outwit the wolf or fight him off on his own. So he went into the stable and untied the colt. Then he called quietly to the wolf, 'Brother Wolf, make sure you bite the hind legs first!'

The wolf obeyed Toby, and the young horse kicked out at him with all its strength, which was exactly what Toby had planned. The wolf leaped to one side, howling and yowling in pain and rage, for the colt's hooves had knackered him badly. He made such a row that the miller heard him, and grabbing his shotgun, he rushed out into the yard and blasted the wolf dead.

Toby sighed with relief as he came out of the stable unharmed. The wolf could lead him into mischief no more and would never trouble him again. For the rest of his puff, Toby could look forward to living happy ever after in the sunshine.

The Juniper Tree

nce upon a time, that very old people can still remember, there lived a man and his good and beautiful wife. They loved each other so much that the only thing they wished for was a little child. Each night before sleep they prayed for a child, but none came and nothing changed.

There was a yard in front of their house and in the centre grew a juniper tree. One winter's day, the wife stood under the juniper tree peeling an apple, and as she was peeling it, she cut her finger and her blood wept onto the snow.

'Oh!' cried the wife, and she sighed deeply. She grew sad as she looked at the tears of blood on the snow. 'If only I had a child as red as blood and as white as snow.' These words seemed to lighten her mood and she felt a glow of cheerfulness as though something might happen. Then she went inside.

After a month, the snow was gone. After two months, everything was green. After three months, the earth grew flowers. After four months, the trees in the forest thickened and their green branches stretched and touched and intertwined. The birds began to sing and their songs tumbled from the trees among the falling blossom. Soon the fifth month had come and gone, and when the wife stood beneath the juniper tree, its sweet scent flooded her heart with happiness and she fell to her knees, pierced with joy. When the sixth month had passed, the fruit was full and swollen and she was serene. In the seventh month, she picked the juniper berries and ate them so obsessively that she became sick and moody. After the eighth month had passed, she pulled her husband to her and wept.

'If I die,' she cried, 'bury me under the juniper tree.'

After that, she was calm and contented until the ninth month was over. Then she had a child as red as blood and as white as snow. But when she looked at her baby for the first time, she was so ecstatic that she died.

Her husband buried her under the juniper tree and wept night and day. As time passed, he began to feel better, but there were still days when he cried. At last, he stopped, and after more suns and moons had gone, he found another wife. Together, he and his second wife had a daughter, while his child from his first wife was a little boy, who was as red as blood and as white as snow. Whenever the woman looked at her daughter, her heart bloomed with love for her. But when she looked at the boy, the same heart jerked with resentment. She knew that he would always be there to get in the way of her daughter inheriting everything. Then the devil gripped her and twisted her feelings towards the boy until she became very cruel to him. She jabbed him from here to there, slapped, slippered, clipped and cuffed him until the poor little boy was living in fear. When he came home after school, his life was hell.

One day, the woman went up to her room and her little girl came after her and asked, '*Mutter*, will you give me an apple?'

'*Ja, meine liebling*,' cooed the woman, and she chose her the most gorgeous apple from the chest, which had a heavy wooden lid and a big sharp iron lock.

'*Mutter*,' said the little daughter, 'shouldn't Brother have one too?'

The woman was annoyed at this, but she said, '*Ja*, when he gets back from school.' And when she looked out of the window and saw the boy coming, the devil tightened his hold on her, and she snatched the apple from her daughter.

'No apples until Brother is here,' she said and she threw the apple into the chest and shut the lid.

The little boy came in and the devil made her be friendly to him and say, 'Would you like a nice apple, *mein liebling*?' But she gave him a murderous look.

'*Mutter*,' said the boy, 'how fierce you look! Yes please, I would like an apple.'

Then something made her entice him.

'Come here, come here,' she coaxed, as she lifted the lid. 'Choose an apple for yourself.'

And as the boy bent over the chest, the devil possessed her, and – *bang!* – she slammed down the lid so hard that his little head flew off and rolled among the apples. The woman went cold with fear and thought, 'How will I get away with this?' She flew up to her room, rushed to her dresser and yanked out a white neckerchief. She balanced the boy's head back on his neck and tied the neckerchief around his throat so that nothing could be seen. Then she propped him in a chair in front of the door and twisted an apple into his hand.

A little while later, little Marlene came into the scullery and tugged at her mother, who was stirring, stirring, stirring a pot of boiling water in front of the fire.

'*Mutter*,' said Marlene, 'Brother is sitting by the door and he has turned very pale. He's got an apple in his hand, but when I asked him to give me the apple he wouldn't reply, and now I'm frightened!'

'Go back to him,' said the woman, 'and if he still won't answer you, give him a good clout on the ear.'

Little Marlene went back to him and said, 'Brother, give me the apple.'

But he said nothing. Nothing. So she fetched him a thump on the ear and his head fell off. The little girl was so terrrified that she began to weep and wail. Then she ran to her Mother and said, 'Oh, *Mutter*, I've knocked my brother's head off.' And she cried and cried and could not be comforted.

'Oh, Marlene,' said the woman, 'what have you done! You'd better keep quiet about this. No one must ever know. And anyway, there's precious little we can do about it now. We'd best make a stew out of him.'

So the mother got the little boy and chopped him into pieces. Then she tossed them into a pot and let them simmer and steam and stew. Marlene stood close by, sobbing, and her tears splashed onto the stew so it did not need any salt.

When the father came home from work, he sat down at the table and asked, 'Where is my son?'

The woman dished up a huge, steamy serving of the stew, and Marlene wept and wept and wept,

'Where's my son?' the father demanded again.

'Oh,' said the woman, 'he's away to the countryside to visit his mother's great uncle. They'll look after him well.'

'Oh, this has upset me,' said the father. 'It's all wrong. He should have said goodbye to me.' Then he began to eat the stew, but said, 'Marlene, what are you blubbing about? Your brother will be home soon enough.' Still munching heartily, he said, 'Wife, this food is delicious! Dish me up some more!' And the more he ate, the more he wanted. 'More!' he said. 'Give me some more! I'm not sharing a scrap of it.

Somehow I feel this has got my name on it!'

As he chomped and chewed, he chucked the bones under the table until he was stuffed. But Marlene slipped to her dresser and fetched her best silk neckerchief from the bottom drawer. She tenderly gathered up all the bones from beneath the table, tied them up in her silk kerchief and carried them outside. Her tears were bitter as she placed the bones beneath the juniper tree. But as she laid them there, she felt suddenly consoled, and the tears dried on her cheeks. And now the juniper tree rustled and moved. The branches parted and joined, parted and joined, as though they were clapping their hands with joy. At the same time, smoke drifted out of the tree, and in the heart of the smoke there was a brightly burning fire. Then a wonderful bird flapped from the flames and began singing beautifully. He soared higher and higher into the air, and when he had disappeared, the juniper tree was just as it was before. But the silk neckerchief was gone. Marlene felt very light and happy. It was as though her brother was still alive, and she went gaily back into the house, sat down at the table, and ate.

Meanwhile, the bird flew away, landed on a

goldsmith's house, and began to sing:

Meine mutter, she killed me.
Mein vater, he ate me.
My sister, Marlene,
Made certain to gather
My bones all together,
In silk wrapped so nicely,
Under the juniper tree.
Tweet-tweet!
Under the juniper tree.
Tweet-tweet!
What a beautiful bird I am!

The goldsmith was busy in his workshop, crafting a golden chain. He heard the bird singing on his roof and thought the sound was beautiful. He stood up to go outside, and as he crossed the threshold he lost a slipper. But he kept on walking, right into the middle of the road, with only one sock and a slipper on. He was also wearing his work apron, and in one hand he held the golden chain and in the other his tongs. The sun sparkled on the street as he walked and then he stopped to get a good look at the bird.

'Bird,' he said, 'you sing so beautifully! Please sing me that song again.'

'No,' said the bird, 'I don't sing twice for nothing. Give me the golden chain and I'll sing it for you once more.'

'It's a deal,' said the goldsmith. 'Here's the golden chain. Now sing that lovely song again.'

The bird swooped down, scooped up the golden chain in his right claw, stood before the goldsmith and began singing:

Meine mutter she killed me.
Mein vater he ate me.
My sister, Marlene,
Made certain to gather
My bones all together,
In silk wrapped so nicely
Under the juniper tree.
Tweet-tweet!
Under the juniper tree.
Tweet-tweet!
What a beautiful bird I am.

Then the bird flapped away to a shoemaker's house, perched on his roof and sang:

Meine mutter she killed me.
Mein vater he ate me.
My sister, Marlene,
Made certain to gather
My bones all together,
In silk wrapped so nicely
Under the juniper tree.
Tweet-tweet!
Under the juniper tree.
Tweet-tweet!
What a beautiful bird I am.

When the shoemaker heard the song, he ran to the door in his singlet and squinted up at the roof, shielding his eyes from the bright sun with his hand.

'Bird,' he said, 'you sing so beautifully!' Then he called into the house. 'Wife! Come outside for a moment. There's a bird up there. Look! He sings so beautifully!' Then he called his daughter and her children, and the apprentices and the maid. They all came hot-footing out into the street to squinny up at the bird, and they saw how truly beautiful he was. He had vivid bright feathers of red and green; his neck glistened like gold, and his eyes sparkled and shone in his head like stars.

'Bird,' said the shoemaker. 'Please sing me that song again.'

'No,' said the bird. 'I don't sing twice for nothing. You'll have to give me a present.'

'Wife,' said the man, 'go into the shop. You'll see a pair of red shoes on the top shelf. Fetch them here.'

His wife hurried and returned with the shoes.

'There you go!' said the man. 'Now sing that lovely song again.'

The bird swooped down, scooped up the shoes in his left claw, flew back onto the roof, and sang:

Meine mutter she killed me.
Mein vater he ate me.
My sister, Marlene,
Made certain to gather
My bones all together,
In silk wrapped so nicely
Under the juniper tree.
Tweet-tweet!
Under the juniper tree.
Tweet-tweet!
What a beautiful bird I am!

When the song was finished, the bird fluttered away. He clutched the gold chain in his right claw and the red shoes in his left, and he flew far away to a mill. *Clickety-clack-clack-clack, clickety-clack-clack-clack* went the mill. The miller had twenty fellows working in the mill, and they were all hewing a millstone. *Chick-chack, chick-chack, chick-chack* went twenty chisels. And the mill kept saying *clickety-clack-clack-clack, clickety-clack-clack-clack*. The bird flew down and perched on a linden tree outside the mill and sang:

Meine mutter she killed me.

the men stopped working.

Mein vater he ate me.

Then two more downed tools and listened.

My sister, Marlene,
Made certain to gather . . .

Then four more stopped.

. . . My bones all together,
In silk wrapped so nicely . . .

Now only eight chaps were chiselling.

. . . Under the juniper tree.
Tweet-tweet!

Now only five.

. . . under the juniper tree.
Tweet-tweet!

Now only one.

What a beautiful bird I am!

Then the last chiseller chucked chiselling and listened
to the final words.

'Bird,' he said, 'you sing so beautifully! Let me hear
it all! Sing your song to me again.'

'No,' answered the bird. 'I don't sing twice for
nothing. Give me the millstone and then I'll sing it
for you again.'

'I would give it to you if I could,' said the man. 'But the millstone doesn't just belong to me.'

'If he sings the song again,' chorused his workmates, 'we'll give him the stone.'

So the bird swooped down and the twenty miller's men grabbed beams to lift the stone. 'Heave-ho! Heave-ho!' The bird pushed his neck through the hole and wore the stone like a collar. Then he flew back to the tree and sang:

Meine mutter she killed me.
Mein vater he ate me.
My sister Marlene
Made certain to gather
My bones all together,
In silk wrapped so nicely,
Under the juniper tree.
Tweet-tweet!
Under the juniper tree.
Tweet-tweet!
What a beautiful bird I am!

The bird finished the song and spread his wings. In his right claw, he had the chain, in his left the shoes, and around his neck the millstone. Then he flew away to the father's house.

The father, the mother and Marlene were sitting at the table in the parlour, and the father cried, 'Hurrah! I'm so happy! I feel absolutely wonderful!'

'I don't, I don't,' said the mother. 'I feel scared, as though a huge storm was brewing.'

Marlene sat there and wept and wept and wept. Then the bird flew over and, as he landed on the roof, the father said, 'Oh, I'm in such a good mood! The sun is shining at its brightest and I feel just as though I were going to meet an old friend again!'

'I don't, I don't,' said his wife. 'I'm so frightened that my teeth are rattling in my head. My blood's in flames in my veins.'

She ripped her bodice from her breast, and Marlene huddled in the corner and wept and wept. She held her handkerchief to her eyes and cried until it was sodden with her tears. The bird swooped down to the juniper tree, where he perched on a branch and began singing:

Meine mutter she killed me.

The Mother covered her ears, squeezed shut her eyes, and tried to see and hear nothing, but there was a roaring in her head like a huge thunderstorm, and her eyes spat and flashed like lightning.

Mein vater he ate me.

'Oh, *Mutter*,' said the Father, 'listen to how beautifully that bird sings. The sun's so warm and it smells of cinammon.'

My sister, Marlene,
Made certain . . .

Marlene put her head on her knees and wept and wept, but the man said, 'I'm going outside. I have to see this bird close-up.'

'Don't go!' gasped the wife. 'I feel as though the whole house is shaking and ready to burst into flames!'

But the man went outside and looked at the bird.

. . . to gather
My bones all together,

In silk wrapped so nicely,
Under the juniper tree.
Tweet-tweet!
Under the juniper tree.
Tweet-tweet!
What a beautiful bird I am!

The bird finished his song and dropped the golden chain so that it fell neatly around the man's neck and fitted him perfectly. The man went inside and said, 'Look how wonderful that bird is! He gave me this gorgeous golden chain and he's just as gorgeous himself!'

But the woman was petrified and collapsed to the floor. Her cap fell from her head and the bird sang again:

Meine mutter, she killed me.

'Aah! I wish I was a thousand feet under the earth and did not have to hear this song!'

Mein vater, he ate me.

Then the woman fell to the floor again as if she was dead.

My sister, Marlene, made certain . . .

'Oh!' said Marlene. 'I want to go outside as well and see if the bird will give me something too!' So she went out.

. . . to gather
My bones all together,
In silk wrapped so nicely . . .

Then the bird threw her the shoes.

. . . under the juniper tree.
Tweet-tweet!
Under the juniper tree.
Tweet-tweet!
What a beautiful bird I am!

Marlene felt light and happy. She slipped her feet into the new red shoes and skipped back into the house.

'Hurrah!' she said 'The bird is so wonderful! He gave

me these red shoes as a present! When I went outside I felt so sad, but now I feel full of joy!'

'I don't, I don't,' gasped the wife. She leapt to her feet and her hair flared and crackled like the red flames of hell. 'I feel as if the end of the world is coming! I must get outside!'

So she rushed out of the door and – *crash!* – the bird threw the millstone down on her head and she was crushed to death. The father and Marlene heard the terrible noise and ran outside. Black smoke and red flames were dancing on the spot, and when it was finished the little brother stood there alive. He took hold of his father's hand and Marlene's hand and the three of them were overjoyed. They went into the house, sat down at the table, and started to eat.

The Girl and the North Wind

igh up in the mountains of Norway a girl lived with her mother. The girl's name was Kari and one day her mother asked her to fetch the flour to bake loaves and biscuits. Kari seized the biggest bowl in the kitchen and ran dutifully to the barn. She filled the bowl right to the top and hurried back across the yard when – *whish-whoosh!* – the North Wind swaggered around the corner and scattered all the flour away with one great puff.

Kari went back to the barn, refilled the bowl, and hastened across the yard when – *whish-whoosh!* – up rushed the North Wind again and blew away all the flour. Yet again Kari went to the barn. She scooped up all the flour that was left, which wasn't even enough to reach halfway up the bowl, and hugged it to her as she bolted across the yard. But – *whish-whoosh!* – around the corner bowled the North Wind and puffed away the flour.

'It'll be gruel for the whole winter now,' scolded Kari's mother. 'There'll be no bread and definitely no biscuits till next year.'

'No bread? No *biscuits*?' gasped Kari. 'Well, I'm going to get the flour back!' And before her mother could draw breath she ran out of the door.

All that day Kari crunched and trudged through the snow until at last she reached the place where the North Wind lived.

'North Wind! Come out here! I want to talk to you! Now!' shouted Kari and she thumped on the door as loudly as she could.

After a few minutes the North Wind opened the door, scratching himself and yawning. 'What's all this banging and bawling? How can I have a decent kip with all this commotion?'

'You stole our flour!' exclaimed Kari. 'You breezed up to our house – *ehn*, *too*, *treh* – three times today and blew away all our flour and now we won't have any bread all winter and we'll probably starve to death and it'll be All Your Fault!'

The North Wind's face puckered and wrinkled. 'I do apologise,' he said in a big blustery voice. 'Sometimes I get completely carried away with blowing. I meant no harm, but it's impossible for me to get your flour back now.' He stared at the girl for a moment. Then he added, 'I can't give you your flour back, but I can give you something else.'

He disappeared inside and returned holding a cloth. 'This cloth is magic. All you have to do is say, "Cloth, cloth, spread yourself and set out scrumptious scram," and you will have all the food and drink you can imagine.'

Kari thanked the North Wind, pocketed the cloth, and set off homewards. It was getting dark, but Kari came to an inn on the road and decided to stay the night there. She knocked on the door and it swung open at once. Out hobbled a troll crone whose warty nose was so long she had tucked it into her waistband to avoid tripping.

'*Goo kuelh*,' rasped the crone in a haggy voice.

'*Goo kuelh*, good evening,' faltered Kari. 'I was wondering, please may I have a bed for the night?'

'How will you pay for it?' growled the troll crone.

'I am afraid I have no money. But I can feed you and your guests.'

'How?'

Kari took out the cloth, gave it a shake, holding it at both ends, and said, 'Cloth, cloth, spread yourself and set out scrumptious scram!'

At once the cloth was groaning with food – soups and soufflés, roasts and stews, steaks and sausages, pies and flans, fruits and vegetables, trifles and puddings, and every kind of drink.

When all the guests at the inn had filled their bellies, Kari rolled up her cloth and went to bed. But at dead of night, when everyone was in the land of nod, the troll crone came creeping up the stairs with a cloth identical to Kari's. She sneaked into her room and swapped her cloth for hers.

Next morning, Kari woke up, snatched the cloth and sprinted all the way home. 'Mama! Mama! Look what the North Wind gave me,' she shouted excitedly. She babbled out the magic words and shook the cloth. Nothing! She tried again – and again – and again – twisting the cloth this way and that, but nothing worked.

'The North Wind has tricked me!' said Kari

furiously and she marched off to the North Wind's house before her mother could say no.

'North Wind! Come outside! I want to talk to you!' bawled Kari at the door. After a while, the North Wind emerged, rubbing his eyes sleepily.

'You again?' he yawned. 'Why are you back so soon?'

'You know very well why I'm back!' yelled Kari, almost in tears. 'The cloth you gave me was useless! It only worked once and what good is that?'

'Just the once? Something is wrong,' said the North Wind. 'But let's not quarrel. I'll give you something else.' Soon enough he came back with an old goat.

'This goat is magic. All you have to do is say, "Goat! Splosh! Crip, crap, dosh!" and it will make all the money you need.'

'Will it work more than once?' asked Kari suspiciously.

'For ever,' promised the North Wind.

So Kari took the goat and set off homewards. It was getting dark so she decided to return to the inn for the night. She knocked on the door and the troll crone swung it open at once. Broth dripped from her huge conk because she'd been using it to stir her souppot.

'Goo *kuelh*, good evening. I was wondering if I could have a bed for tonight?' said Kari.

'How are you going to pay?' rattled the crone.

Kari turned to the old goat and said, 'Goat! Splosh! Crip, crap, dosh!' Immediately, out of its backside, dropped a jackpot of gold coins. Kari paid the crone, used another sovereign for food and drink, and then went to bed. In the middle of the night, the troll crone once more came crawling up the stairs, this time with her own goat, which she switched for Kari's.

When Kari got home next day, she tried to show her mother just what the goat could do. But whatever came out of *this* old goat's rear end was stinking but not rich!

Kari stomped back to the North Wind, more livid than ever. The North Wind just scratched at his flowing silvery mane, tossed it, and said, 'Something is wrong. I'll give you one last thing, but you'd better use it wisely.' Off he went and back he came with a stick. 'This stick is magic. All you have to do is say "Stick, stick, lay on!" and it will thrash anyone you want. When you want it to stop, just say "Stick, stick, lay off!" and it will come straight back to you.'

Kari thanked the North Wind and went straight to the Inn.

'*Goo kuelh*,' cawed the troll crone.

'May I have a bed for the night?'

'How do you plan to pay?' growled the crone, leering at the stick. Kari found some spare coins in her apron and went straight to bed.

In the dark small hours, the crone came creeping up the stairs again. She was certain the stick was magic. Slowly she sneaked into the room. Just as she was about to swap her stick for Kari's, up Kari jumped and bellowed, 'Stick, stick, lay on!'

The stick whizzed from the pillow and began to give the troll crone such a hiding that she danced from one foot to the other all over the room, howling and hooting and hollering, until at last she screeched, 'Make it stop! Make it stop!'

'Not until you give me back my cloth and my goat,' shouted Kari.

'I will, I will!' shrieked the troll crone.

'Stick, stick, lay off,' ordered Kari and at once the stick flew – *whish-whoosh!* – into her hand. But she kept a firm grip on it as she marched behind the troll crone to fetch her cloth and her goat.

The next morning, Kari ran home with her treasures, and with them she and her mother had all the food and money and protection they needed for the rest of their long and extremely happy lives.

Snipp, snapp, snute,
Her er eventyret ute!
Snip, snap, snut,
My gob's now shut!

Rats and the Chinese Zodiac

ats!

Members of the genus *rattus* –
black or brown –
Found in countryside and town.
Long-tailed rodents, live in packs;
Collective noun, *mischief* of Rats.
Blamed for the fleas upon their backs
Who brought the plague in the Middle Ages
On the ships that sailed to here from Asia.
Unfair!

Rats!
Expert jumpers, climbers, swimmers.
Love their food – they're no slimmers!
The second most successful mammal

On the planet? Fact – the Rat!
They go where you go – gnawing, chewing.
No Rat is ever more than ten feet from a human.

Rats!

Colour-blind. Fantastic sense of smell.
From their whiskers they can tell
Exactly where they are – how far, how near.
They can disappear down a sewer, down a well.
Rats are clever, sociable, untemperamental.
In India, they have their very own and sacred Hindu
temple!

Rats!

Who can say why cats chase Rats?
It's all to do with the Chinese Zodiac.

A long, long time ago when the world was still young,
all the creatures on the planet were good friends
and true comrades. Everyone liked everyone else
and there was never any trouble. In fact, although
you might find this hard to believe, the Cat and the

Rat were so close and were such terrific pals that they shared a house. One day, it was announced that all the animals in China were invited to enter a competition to win a place in the twelve signs of the Zodiac. There was going to be a long and hard race and the winner would become the first sign of the Zodiac; the second would become the second sign of the Zodiac; the third would become the third sign of the Zodiac; the fourth would . . . Well, it's quite obvious how matters were to be arranged. The animals were incredibly excited about this wonderful opportunity, but the Cat and the Rat were anxious. The thing was, they were both addicted to sleeping, snoozing and snoring, and they were very worried that they would miss the start of the big race. The Cat and the Rat discussed this mutual problem at considerable length before deciding to ask their friend, the Ox, to make quite sure that they woke up in good time for the off. The loyal Ox agreed and gave his solemn word.

So – the day of the great race dawned and the Ox made his way to the home of the Cat and the Rat while the dew was still wet on the cherry blossom. *Bang! Bang! Bang!* he went on the front door with his great big mighty hoof – but there was no reply! *Bellow! Bellow! Bellow!* he roared at the window with his great big mighty voice – but there was no reply! So the Ox broke down the door with his great big mighty shoulder and barged into the bedroom to meet the Cat and the Rat as he had promised.

Would you credit it? The two bone-idle specimens were so deeply asleep in their stinking pit that nothing the Ox did could wake them up (and he tried *everything*!) The Ox saw that it was getting late, so he picked up the Cat and the Rat, put them on his great big mighty back, and made his way to the start of the race. *On your marks! Get set! Go!*

The race began and the Ox ran as fast as he could, still with the Cat and the Rat in the land of Nod on his broad back. If the Ox could *win* the race, then all three of the gang would be part of the Zodiac! Of course, all the bouncing up and down on top of the Ox at last woke up the Rat!

He looked across and there was the Cat, still kipping away, and the Rat suddenly had a brainwave! If the Cat were to wake up and start running, there was totally no way the Rat could beat her. The Cat was so much bigger and faster than the Rat. So he gave the Cat a good shove and she fell straight off the back of the Ox! The poor Cat bounced twice on the ground, rolled into the ice-cold river and was at once wide awake! She splashed and crawled her way out of the water just in time to see all the other animals racing past her and speeding away. The Ox was almost at the finishing line when the Rat climbed up on to his head – and just before the Ox broke the tape to win the race, the Rat jumped forwards as far as he possibly could and managed to beat the Ox by a whisker!

This is why the Rat is the first sign of the Chinese Zodiac (and the Ox is the second). But as for the Cat, she never forgave the Rat for pushing her off the Ox's back and into the river. To this very day, instead of being good friends, true comrades and sharing a home, Cats chase Rats as soon as they see them. Like this!

The Pied Piper of Hamelin

I n your ancestors' time in the town of Hamelin, which is still there, there was an invasion of rats the like of which it is impossible for us to imagine, but we will try. These rats were dirty great black things, which ran as they pleased in broad daylight through the streets and swarmed all over the houses so that folk couldn't put their hand or foot down without touching something furry. When dressing in the morning they found rats in their underpants and petticoats, in their hats, boots, briefcases and pockets. One poor citizen had found two rats playing in her brassiere.

When anyone wanted a bite to eat, the rats had been there first! The Cook, for example, was always going into her larder and finding that the rats had eaten the cheese or sucked the eggs or nibbled the bread or gnawed the rind off the best bacon. The Cook had a good moan about it to the Priest, who agreed with her, because he had found rats in the pockets of his cassock, and had had his King James Bible chewed from Genesis to Revelations. In fact, there was nowt left of his Holy Candle but the wick!

The Priest had a right old bitch about it with the Poet, who agreed with him because she couldn't write poetry any more on account of the noise. As soon as it got dark, the rats set to work, nibbling away from cellar to garret. Everywhere, in the ceilings, in the floors, in the cupboards, at the doors, there was a scamper and a rummage, and such a furious noise of gimlets, pincers and saws, that the Poet was a nervous wreck! So the townsfolk agreed to march to the Town Hall and find the Politician to demand that something was done about the bloody rats.

The Politician announced that they were all in this together and he would launch an Official Inquiry . . . but at this everyone plonked themselves down on their bottoms and refused to budge until the Politician came up with a better idea.

Well, they sat there from noon till dusk while the Politician consulted his Moral Compass and looked at his Legacy and mentioned his Mandate, when there arrived in the town a man with an unusual face, who played on a pipe and sang these words:

'If you live, you'll see
This is me –
I was born to be
The Rat-catcher!'

He was an odd, gawky person, very weatherbeaten, with a long crooked nose, a droopy rat-tail moustache, and two great yellow piercing eyes under a felt hat with a crimson feather. He was dressed in a green jacket, red pantaloons and big leather boots. He stopped outside the Town Hall, with his back to the Church, and continued with his music, singing:

'If you live, you'll see
This is me –
I was born to be
The Rat-catcher!'

The Politician came rushing from the Town Hall, followed by the citizens, and the Pied Piper explained that if they made it worth his while, he would get rid of all their rats, right down to the last one.

'He's not from round here!' cried the citizens with one voice. 'He might trick us! We can't trust him!'

But the Politician knew a potential vote-winner when he saw one! He was determined that it was high time everyone went home and stopped blaming him for the rats. So he said, 'I give you my word of honour, Piper, that you will be properly rewarded, should you succeed in ridding our town of rats. How much do you charge?'

'By midnight tonight, I shall remove every rat from this place, if you promise to pay me one gold sovereign per head.'

'One gold sovereign for each rat!' cried the citizens with one voice. 'But that will come to millions of pounds!'

But despite the grumbling of the people, the Politician was not for turning. He shook hands with the Piper, gave him a beaming smile, and guaranteed to pay him one gold sovereign per head with the taxpayers' own money.

The Piper replied that he would start this evening when the moon rose. He requested that the inhabitants leave the streets empty, but said that they could look out of their windows at what was happening and that it would be an interesting event. And so, at about nine o'clock that night, the Pied Piper reappeared by the Town Hall, back to the Church, and as the moon rose on the horizon, he began to play on his pipe.

At first the music was slow and dreamy, gentle as a caress; but then it grew more and more lively as though

it was saying, 'Come and dance!' It could be heard loud and clear in the farthest alley of the town. Soon, from the depths of the cellars and sewers, from the tops of the attics and garrets, from out of the larders, cupboards, wardrobes, handbags and wellingtons, from under the beds and tables, from every corner of every house or shop . . . out came the rats! They ran out of the doors, jumped into the street and tap, tap, tap, began to dance, all squeezed together, towards the Town Hall. There were so many of them they looked like a filthy flood in full flow.

When the square was completely rammed, the Piper turned away and, still playing wonderfully, magically, began to walk towards the river at the foot of the town. The rats followed eagerly until the Piper stopped playing and pointed to the middle of the river where the water was flowing and swirling and foaming and whirling dangerously.

'Hop! Hop!' he cried. 'Hop! Hop!' And straight away, without pausing for a moment, the rats began to jump in, head first, one after another, and disappeared. It was almost midnight when, at the very end of the line, crawling along slowly, came a big old rat, silver with age. It was the boss of the plague.

'Are they all in, my old friend?' asked the Piper.

'They are all in, brother,' replied the silver rat.

'And how many were there?'

'Nine hundred and ninety thousand, nine hundred and ninety-nine.'

'Including you?'

'Including me!'

'Then go and join them, old friend, till we meet again.'

Then the silver rat jumped into the river and disappeared.

The Piper had kept his end of the bargain and went off to his bed at the inn. And for the first time in a long, long while, the citizens of Hamelin slept peacefully through the night and the Poet was able to start at last on a new poem.

The next morning, just after nine o'clock, the Pied Piper arrived outside the Town Hall, where all the well-rested and breakfasted citizens had already gathered and were cheering and applauding the Politician.

'All your rats went for a swim in the river last night,' called out the Piper, 'and I guarantee not one will return. There were nine hundred and ninety thousand, nine hundred and ninety-nine, at one gold sovereign a head. It is time to count out my wages.'

'Just a moment, stranger,' smiled the Politician. One sovereign a head means one head a sovereign. Where are the heads?'

The taxpayers roared with laughter, but the Piper had not expected this devious ploy. He shook with rage and his eyes burned red.

'The heads?' he hissed. 'If you want the heads, then go and find them in the river!'

'Oh, I see!' boomed the Politician confidently. 'You are refusing to keep to the terms of our arrangement. One sovereign per head. Where are the heads?'

The crowd joined in with one voice: 'Where are the heads? Where are the heads? Show us the heads!'

'Order! Order!' cried the Politician, in charge once more. He turned to the Piper and said, 'We could refuse even to pay you a penny. But we are a Big Society and you have been of use to us. Why not accept a token ten sovereigns for your trouble, before you leave?'

'Keep your token ten sovereigns,' replied the Piper poisonously. 'If you do not pay me, I will be paid by your children.'

Then he pulled his hat down over his eyes, turned

away, and left the town without speaking to a soul.

The taxpayers gave high-fives and slapped each other on the back and laughed when the Politician said the Rat-catcher had been caught in his own trap. But what made them laugh most of all was his threat of passing their debt onto their children.

The next day was a Sunday and they all went happily to the Church, looking forward to a Sunday lunch after Mass that hadn't been sampled by rats.

But when everyone returned home to his or her house, their children had gone.

'Our children! Where are our children?' was the terrible cry that was heard in every street.

Then, limping from the east side of the town, came a little lame boy who was sobbing loudly and this is what he told . . .

While all the adults were at Church, a wonderful music had started. Soon, all the boys and girls who had been left safely at home had run outside, following the magical sound to the square by the Town Hall. They found the Pied Piper there, playing his music just as he had on the night he caught all the rats. Then the Piper had walked quickly towards the east gate of the town and all the children had followed, running, singing, clapping, dancing to the music, as far as the foot of the mountain outside Hamelin. But when they got near, the mountain had opened and the Piper had gone in, still playing his music, and all the children had danced after him, after which the mountain had closed again. The only child left was the lame boy who could not keep up with the others.

When they heard this story, the parents wailed in horror and distress. They ran with sledgehammers and pikes to the mountain, and banged at the rock till darkness, searching for the opening. The Politician, who had lost three little boys and two little girls, clawed at the stone with bloodied hands, but it was all useless. When night fell, the citizens had to return to Hamelin without their children, and only the cold face of the moon was witness to the dreadful sights and sounds of their grief.

The Stolen Childhood

stepmother lived with her dead husband's young daughter. The girl was sweet-natured and lovely, but the stepmother had a heart that had soured and shrivelled under her black frock. Her hair had dried and rusted on her head and she took pleasure in nothing.

Day after day, she watched her stepdaughter as she played in the garden and the stepmother's blood clogged with envy as she saw the young girl chasing butterflies or turning cartwheels or singing to herself in the arms of the apple tree. More than anything, the stepmother yearned and burned to be young again.

One day, a stranger came to the town and took a room at the inn. The stepmother, staring as usual from her window, noticed the stranger walking in the lane. He was tall and dark and as the woman gazed down at him, he glanced up and spied her. With one look he saw into her dark soul and knew what she wanted.

'Come to me,' he said, and she heard him and jumped, as though a poker were stirring the burnt coals and ashes of her heart. She hurried outside into the lane to stand beside him.

Close up she could see that there was no kindness in his face and she shivered. He was holding a pair of sharp silver scissors.

'I can give you what you most want,' he said. 'Take these scissors and cut the shadow from the first young person you find asleep. Then you must snip off your own shadow and throw it over the young person without waking them. Their youth will be yours at once and they will be as old as you are now.'

'What must I pay you for this?' asked the stepmother, because she knew very well there would be a price.

'You will be my bride,' he answered, 'on the happiest day of your life.'

The stepmother gave a dry laugh and thought that the man was joking, but she agreed to his strange bargain and took the scissors. He walked rapidly away down the lane and quite soon after that he left the town.

The stepmother went into the garden holding the scissors, which glittered in her hand in the sunlight.

Her young stepdaughter was stretched out on the lawn with her straw hat over her face, fast asleep in the warm buttery sun. Her shadow lay on the grass beside her, so cool and dark that already the daisies there had started to close.

The stepmother knelt down, silent as poison, and cut along the whole length of the girl's shadow. A breeze blew under it and lifted it gently, but the stepmother snatched at it, crumpling it up and stuffing it in her skirt pocket. It felt like the softest silk.

Then the stepmother stood and saw her own long shadow at her feet. She bent down and with a *snap!* and a *snip!* she cut it off. She lifted her heavy, leathery shadow and tossed it over the sleeping girl, then turned and ran towards the house to look in the mirror. Her step felt lighter and for the first time in years she noticed all the different smells of the garden as she ran.

The stepdaughter felt something heavy and

sour-smelling upon her and opened her eyes in fright. It was dark. She screamed and tried to jump up but her body felt stiff and strange and her back ached.

She sat up and pushed the shadow away from her and it lay in a heap like an old black coat.

'How horrible!' cried the girl.

She touched her throat. Her voice was different, deeper and harsher, not like a child's voice at all. She looked at her hands. They were like a pair of crumpled gloves, several sizes too big, the skin loose and creased over the bones.

She stood up slowly, holding the small of her back, and heard the waxy creak of her knees. Truly scared now, she hurried as fast as she could, a bit out of breath, to look in the mirror.

The mirror was a full-length one and hung in the shadowy hall. The stepmother was standing before it and she turned her head as she heard the sound of her stepdaughter behind her. Both of them stared at each other in disbelief and then the stepmother began to laugh, the light easy laugh of a young girl.

'Look at yourself!' she cried and pulled her stepdaughter to the mirror.

A middle-aged face stared back from the glass,

grey-haired and lined. The stepdaughter's teeth felt strange and uncomfortable in her mouth and when she touched them with her tongue she realised that they were false. She began to cough and the bitter taste of tobacco scalded the back of her throat. She turned to her stepmother.

Her stepmother was smaller, with soft hair the colour of a conker and skin as delicate as the petal of a rose. She was jumping up and down and clapping her hands.

'It worked! It worked!' she cried. 'I am young again and *you* have all my years!'

Then the stepmother spun round and ran back into the sunshine and the poor stepdaughter fell to the floor in the dark hall and sobbed bitterly.

Summer turned, as it has to do, into autumn and autumn soon became winter.

It was the stepdaughter now who stood at the window, a shawl round her cold stiff bones, watching the village children throw snowballs in the field on the other side of the lane.

She wondered why her young stepmother never played with the others, why she never helped to make a snowman – pushing a snowball along till it doubled and trebled and quadrupled in size, creaking under her mittens. And why she never hopped and whistled her way to school with the other children or pressed her nose to the toyshop window or scraped a stick along the green railings of the park. What was the point of her stepmother being young at all?

A fierce headache tightened round her brow, deepening the frowns and creases on her papery skin, and she turned away from the window and went to lie down on the bed in her hushed, dull room. She was always tired now.

She took out her teeth and put them in a glass of water on the bedside table. They grinned away at her as though Death himself had come to call.

But downstairs the stepmother pulled on her boots and went for a walk in the snow, ignoring the shouts of the children playing in the field.

'Youth,' she sneered to herself, 'is wasted on the young.'

She walked for miles, breathing in the clean cold air and not feeling the faintest bit tired, working up a good hunger for dinner.

She grabbed a fistful of snow and sucked at it, gasping at the cold. She was young again! Young!

Her skin and her eyes and her hair sparkled in the hard white winter light.

Winter turned to spring then summer then autumn then winter then spring then summer . . .

The stepmother was taller now and beautiful and many young men came to the house to visit her. They brought flowers and perfume and chocolates and told her that they adored her, and that she was the loveliest young girl in the village, that her lips were rubies and her eyes were sapphires and that each little nail on the tips of her fingers was a pearl.

'I am in the springtime of my life,' gloated the stepmother. 'Again!'

Her stepdaughter watched the young men come and go from her window, but none of them so much as glanced up at the sad old woman with the dull eyes and the yellowing teeth.

One young man, the stepdaughter thought, was handsomer and jollier than all the rest, and her heart, tired as it was, would skip a beat as though it had almost remembered something, whenever she saw him.

At night she would dream that she was dancing and laughing in his arms, a girl once more. But when she woke up she was alone, brittle and aching in the mothbally shroud of her nightgown.

As the summer passed, she noticed that the young man came more and more often to the house to visit her stepmother and that the other boys had drifted away.

On the first day of autumn her stepmother and the young man came before her and told her that they were to be married. Her tired heart sank like a stone in her chest as she looked at the young man and she knew then that she loved him, but she kissed her stepmother and wished her happiness.

'Oh, I will be happy,' answered the stepmother. 'My wedding day will be the happiest day of my life.'

The stepmother had decided to be married at Christmas. The days fell from the calendar like leaves from the trees and, quicker than the snip of scissors, it was the morning of Christmas Eve.

The wedding was to be at noon and already the bellringers were swinging from their ropes, sending the warm bronze voices of the bells across the frozen fields. The bride was to be driven from the house to the church in a white carriage pulled by a chestnut horse. The stepdaughter was to ride behind her in a plain wooden carriage.

As the bells chimed eleven o'clock, the stepdaughter was standing in the lane waiting for the carriages to arrive. The cold bit through her dark winter coat into her bones.

'Here I am!' Her stepmother stood at the door of the house in a dress of silver and gold. 'How do I look?'

'You look good enough to eat,' said a harsh voice from the lane.

The stepdaughter saw the shock and surprise on her stepmother's face and turned to see who had spoken.

A tall man with a mean face and fierce eyes had appeared from nowhere and stood staring intensely at the bride. 'Our carriage will soon be here.'

'Our carriage?' said the stepmother. 'You must be mistaken!'

All the colour had drained from her face until she was paler than the late white roses that she carried in her hands.

'Come,' said the stranger impatiently. 'You know very well what is to happen today.'

'Today is to be the happiest day of my life,' replied

the stepmother in a trembling voice. 'I am to marry the young man who loves me.'

'You are to marry me, my beauty,' said the tall man, 'and you can forget about love. Come!'

'Marry you?' said the bride. 'You?' She laughed hysterically.

The sound of horses' hooves clattered suddenly in the lane and the stepmother ran to her stepdaughter and clutched at her arm. She had started to cry and the stepdaughter could see that she was shaking with fear.

'Who is he?' she asked the terrified bride.

The carriages had arrived, but one was a closed ebony carriage drawn by four black horses who steamed and snorted in the lane.

'Get into the carriage!' said the stranger as he flung open the door.

'No! No! You can't make me!' The stepmother was sobbing now and quite wild with terror and the stepdaughter felt real dread, colder than ice, chilling her heart.

'Who is he? Tell me!' she said again.

'For the last time,' said the man, 'get into the carriage.'

But the stepmother looked into his eyes and saw all the badness of this world and the next and would not go. She shook her head.

The stranger gave a twisted smile and stared hard at the bride.

'You have broken your promise,' he said. 'Put your hand in the pocket of your dress.'

The stepmother did as she was told and pulled out a small piece of crumpled black silk. She gave a little scream and dropped it, and it floated down to the ground and landed at her stepdaughter's feet.

Then the tall man pulled off his coat and the stepdaughter saw that it was the old black coat that had nearly suffocated her when she was a child. With a quick movement the stranger threw it over her stepmother, completely covering her lovely gold and silver dress.

'Don't!' she screamed. 'I'll come! I'll come!'

'Too late,' said the man, and he climbed into the ebony carriage. The four black horses tossed their heads and neighed and began to move away.

'Come back!' screeched the stepmother, but the carriage gathered speed, reached the bend at the top of the lane and vanished. The clatter of hooves faded into the distance.

The stepmother flung away the coat and turned to face her stepdaughter. 'Help me!' she said. 'What am I to do?'

Her stepdaughter was staring at her in horror. The stepmother's beautiful dress hung in tattered grey rags from her bony shoulders. Her hair had turned white and clumps of it had fallen from her head, leaving some of it bald. Her mouth had shrunk inwards in a small wrinkled O of disappointment, as though her lips were mourning her vanished teeth. Her body shrivelled and stooped till she looked like a question mark asking, *Why? Why? Why?*

She was five times as old as before and her voice when she spoke was the dusty croak of a crone. 'Why do you stare at me?'

Then she clutched at her throat and gaped at her stepdaughter. Colour had flooded back into the stepdaughter's hair, a glowing red-blonde, and the girl was smiling at her with perfect white teeth.

'What is happening to me?' she said, and when she heard the light music of her own voice she laughed with delight. 'Stepmother! I am myself again!'

She felt her young lungs breathing easily and her

heart opened like a flower in her breast.

There were running footsteps in the lane and it was the bridegroom, out of breath and looking for the bride. He glanced curiously at the old witch, bent double by the ditch, coughing and cursing, but as soon as he saw the girl he had eyes only for her.

'Your bride has gone,' she said to him.

'I am sorry to hear that,' he said politely, but his eyes burned with sudden love as he looked at her.

There was a strange noise from the ditch and they both turned to see the old black coat lying in a heap on the road. There was no sign of the stepmother, but a sudden gust of wind blew a handful of ashes, grey and gritty, over the fields.

'Your bride has gone for ever,' repeated the girl.

'My bride was lovely,' said the young man, 'but you are truly the most beautiful girl I have ever seen in my life.'

The girl looked down at her hands and saw the light of youth that glowed under her skin and she felt the force and energy of life itself rise up from the tingling tips of her toes so that all she wanted to do was run!

'Catch me if you can!' She laughed at the young

man and took to her heels, flinging off her heavy winter coat as she went.

With a shout, laughing himself, he chased her, never quite catching her, his pounding feet landing on her slim fast shadow as she ran before him.

A Little Girl

 Little Girl lived with her little family in a Doll's House.

There was Little Grandma, who had her own room at the top of the house.

There was Little Grandad, who dozed in a rocking chair in front of the fire all day, even in summer.

There was Little Mother, who spent most of her time in the kitchen, cooking.

And there was Little Twin, the Little Girl's twin sister, who shared her bedroom and slept above the Little Girl in the top bunk.

Every morning, the little family would eat breakfast together in the kitchen and Little Mother would serve tiny boiled eggs in teeny egg cups and the weeniest glasses of orange juice.

After breakfast, Little Grandma would climb up the stairs to her room, sit on a little chair and stare out of the window.

Little Grandad rocked himself slowly to sleep in front of the orange and crimson fire while Little Mother tidied away the breakfast things; and the Little Girl and her Little Twin went to the drawing room to play on the little upright piano or read wee books or dance together. The afternoons ticked away, the two children throwing a red ball between them, the size of a berry. Every day was the same and, whenever the Little Girl asked to go outside, her mother shushed her or her grandparents tutted or her sister shook her head.

At night, when the house grew dark, tiny lamps came on in the Doll's House and the little family sat together round the fire until it was time for bed. Then the Little Girl lay in her bottom bunk with her eyes wide open, listening to the thick deep silence of the darkness.

One morning, the Little Girl looked across at her Little Twin and noticed that she seemed smaller. The Little Girl thought that perhaps she was imagining this, but her own tiny black shoes no longer fitted and she had to go about the house barefooted since they were her only pair.

When she sat down for breakfast, she found that her chair was too small for her and her knees scraped on the underside of the kitchen table. She was still hungry after she'd eaten her boiled egg and toast and still thirsty after she'd drained her weeny glass of orange juice, but nobody else seemed to notice these things, so the Little Girl said nothing.

Later, when she asked whether she might go outside, her mother shushed her and her grandparents tutted and her sister shook her head. That night, as she lay in her bunk, her feet poked out from under her blankets and her head pressed hard against the wall behind her pillow, so she gathered her bedclothes together and stretched out on the floor till morning came.

When the light from outside arrived, she sat up to discover that her head was at the same height as her Little Twin's bunk bed.

Little Twin started to cry as she looked at her sister's large, pale face, a breathing moon, then she ran downstairs to the kitchen, calling for Little Mother.

From then on, the Little Girl grew apart from the rest of her family. They looked at her strangely as she squeezed herself through the little doors of the Doll's House or stooped and knelt to avoid banging her head on the ceilings.

They complained bitterly when they found that she had eaten the entire contents of their little fridge to satisfy her hunger. They whispered to themselves when she knocked over the furniture as she passed.

Curled in the attic, the largest space in the house, the Little Girl heard the fierce squeaks of her family's voices far below. She lifted her arms above her head, carefully raised the red-tiled roof of the Doll's House and climbed outside.

Now that she could stand at her full height, the Little Girl saw that she was as tall as the Doll's House. The chimneys looked like boxes of matches; the front door like a cigarette packet. The windows seemed no bigger than playing cards. She put her eye to the glass of her grandmother's room. Little Grandma sat in her chair staring out through her window, still and unblinking. She looked, the Little Girl thought, just like a wax doll.

She knelt down and peered in through the

drawing-room window. Little Grandad was asleep in his rocking chair in front of the orange and crimson fire, which never burned down.

Her sister, Little Twin, was reading the same page of a wee book over and over again.

The Little Girl's eyes filled with tears, which fell and splashed against the window like rain.

She stretched out and leaned on her elbow to peep

through the kitchen window where Little Mother stood at the table ready to tidy away the breakfast things. More than anything, the Little Girl wished that for once her mother would put on the teeny hat and weeny coat that hung from the hook on the kitchen door, walk out of the kitchen, along the hall and out through the front door.

All day, she stared and peeped and squinted through the windows of the Doll's House, noticing the bath the size of a soap dish, the piano the size of a mouth organ, the fridge the size of a choc ice. That night, the Little Girl lay down on the floor outside the Doll's House. She could see the tiny lights go out inside the house as she drifted away into sleep.

When she awoke, she was even bigger than before. There was a big comfy-looking bed with plump pillows in the room she was in, a large wooden wardrobe full of clothes, which fitted her perfectly, and several pairs of shoes that were just the right size for her feet. She chose a lovely red dress and a pink pair of soft leather boots.

Delicious cooking smells were coming from below. Her Tall Mother smiled at her as she entered the kitchen and said that they'd be having breakfast in the garden. The kitchen window was open and the whole wide wonderful world stretched endlessly away in the morning sunlight.

So the girl grew and grew and the Doll's House stayed in the corner of her bedroom. She peeped in through its windows at first, but soon she forgot to do this, for she had her own big windows now and she could see the stars.

She went outside whenever she wished and travelled far and wide under the sun and under the moon. In time, she went to live in another house and the Doll's House was packed away and forgotten. She became a woman and had her own family and, though she had her troubles from time to time as everyone does, she was very happy for many years.

One day, the woman looked in the mirror and saw that she had become old. There were silver threads in her hair and fine lines on her face. Her own daughter had grown now and had long since moved away and her son was a man who lived in a distant country.

One day, she went up to the attic to store some apples that needed ripening and saw, tucked away in a corner, the old Doll's House.

She knelt before it and peered in through one of the

upstairs windows. Little Grandma was sitting in her chair, staring sightlessly out. The woman's heart gave a horrible lurch and her breath came out in a gasp, covering the window with a fine mist. She rubbed at the glass with a corner of her sleeve and Little Grandma stared right through her just as before.

Then the old woman looked into the window of her old bedroom and saw that both the little bunk beds were empty, so she crouched lower and peeped into the drawing-room window.

Little Twin sat quietly, reading a wee book, and Little Grandad was asleep in the rocking chair in front of the orange and crimson fire.

The woman tapped on the pane with her fingernail but Little Twin didn't look up from her wee book and Little Grandad slept on.

The woman felt herself shrinking with longing and regret.

She moved her head till it was level with the kitchen window. Little Mother stood at the table as she always had. The woman's heart brimmed with love, like a glass filling with the finest wine, and without thinking she banged hard on the glass with her fists.

Then Little Mother was waving and smiling at her

and had run down the hall to fling open the front door and she felt her Little Twin's tiny hand in hers, pulling her inside, and heard the small excited clucks of Little Grandma and Little Grandad as they walked towards her. The door closed behind her with a small click.

That night the Little Girl stood at her bedroom window as her little family slept. Outside the Doll's House, planets glowed and shone like giant apples far out in the endless universe.

The Maiden with No Hands

 King once became a widower and had no wife by his side. He fretted and sulked about this until the Devil put it into his head that he should marry his own sister. Her name was Penta. The selfish, spoilt King sent for Penta one day and said, 'Sister, a man of good judgement never allows anything valuable to leave his house. Plus, you never know what might occur if a stranger were to show up. I know you very well, your character and so on, and I value you, of course, so I have decided you shall be my next wife and must settle down to the business of being a useful partner to me. There! Just what the doctor ordered.'

When Penta heard these outrageous words she was shocked to the core and thought her brother must be mad. She went red in the face and exclaimed, 'Are you out of your tiny mind? I can't believe what you've just suggested. If it's meant to be funny, it's foolhardy! If it's meant to be serious, it's stupid! If it's meant to be practical, it's pathetic! We are brother and sister, you cuckoo! Pay attention! If my virtuous ears ever hear such words again from your slimy tongue, I'll do something to surprise you! If you do not treat me like a sister, then I shall not treat you as a brother!'

Penta fled to her room, locked and bolted the door behind her, and did not see her brother for a whole month. The wretched King was left to skulk around as though his face had been walloped by a sledgehammer. He was as furtive as a boy who has smashed a window and as confused as a cook who has seen the dog run off with the sausages. Nevertheless, when Penta eventually appeared, he was at it again, trying to persuade her to go into partnership as a wife because he was a lonely widower.

'No, no, no, no, no,' said Penta. 'I'm your sister! What is it about me that could possibly make you think I could be your wife?'

'Penta,' replied the King, 'it is your hands! Like forks

they draw out the core of my heart from my chest. Like hooks they lift the bucket of my soul from the well of my being. Like pincers they grip my spirit tightly while love smooths it like a file. Oh, hands! Beautiful hands! They are ladles spooning out sweetness! They are pliers extracting promises! They are shovels digging in my consciousness!'

Hearing this claptrap, Penta told him to be quiet, even though he wanted to say more. 'I've heard enough,' she said. 'Stay there and don't go away. I'll be right back.'

She went to her room, called a servant who was as daft as a banana, gave him a knife and some gold, and said to him, 'Boy, cut my hands off. I want to give them a special manicure.'

The servant thought he was doing her a favour and cut her hands off – *chop! chop!* – with two clean blows. Penta had them put in a bowl and covered with a cloth, then sent to her brother with a message telling him to enjoy the hands that he admired so much and wishing him a good life. The King was livid. He had a trunk built and smeared with tar. Then he ordered his sister to be pushed inside and thrown into the sea.

The trunk was tossed about by the waves, then landed on a beach where some fishermen sorting their nets discovered it. They were amazed to find the beautiful Penta inside. One of the men was also the chief of the island and he took her home and told his wife to be kind to her. But the fishwife was jealous of Penta's beauty and bundled her back into the trunk and launched it into the sea.

The trunk was swallowed up by the waves and battered about back and forth until it was spotted by a ship in which a foreign King was sailing. He had

a boat lowered into the water to fetch the trunk and bring it on board. When it was opened and the kind King saw such a living beauty in that coffin of death he swore he had found great treasure, even if it was a casket of jewels without handles. He took Penta to his kingdom and gave her as a lady-in-waiting to the Queen. Penta served her as well as she could with her feet, even cooking for her, threading needles, ironing her dresses, and combing her hair. The Queen grew as fond of Penta as though she were her own daughter.

But sadly, after a while the Queen grew ill and knew she had to die. She was resigned to this and told her husband that if he loved her and wanted her to be happy in death, he must promise her to marry Penta after the Queen closed her eyes and turned to dust.

The King said, 'I hope you live another hundred years, my darling. However if you must go to that other world and leave me in darkness, I swear to you that I will take Penta for my wife. I don't care that she has no hands so long as I give you a sign of how much I love you in death.' And after the Queen had extinguished the candle of her days, he kept his promise and Penta was soon expecting a child.

The King had to undertake another journey by sea and he said goodbye to Penta and set sail. Nine months later, Penta gave birth to a dazzling boy and the whole kingdom was lit up. The King's advisers sent him a letter bearing this wonderful news, but the ship carrying the letter was caught up in a storm and washed up on the beach where the fishermen had first found Penta in the trunk. The wife who had betrayed Penta was walking there and asked the ship's captain where he was headed. The captain told her everything about the King marrying Penta the Handless and that he must deliver a letter containing great news concerning Penta to the King. Hearing this, the treacherous fishwife invited the captain for a drink and deliberately set out to get him drunk. As soon as he passed out, she found the letter in his pocket. When she read about the baby, she was consumed with envy. She forged another letter saying that Penta had given birth to a little dog, and that the King's advisers were awaiting the King's orders. She swapped the letters and put the false one back in the captain's pocket.

When he awoke – with an awful hangover – and saw the weather had improved, he set sail again to deliver the letter to the King. The King replied at once, instructing his advisers to cheer up the Queen and tell her that these things happened. She was not to have a moment's regret because such matters were ordained by heaven and no human being could influence the stars!

He sent the captain on his way and the gullible captain decided to drop anchor at the beach and visit the fishwife for another drink. Once more she filled him with booze so that he passed out. She read the King's letter and replaced it with a false one which ordered the royal advisers to burn the mother and son as soon as they read it.

But when the forgery reached them, the King's advisers, those wise old men, discussed it for a long time, murmuring and pondering. They concluded that the King was either crazy or bewitched, because he had a pearl of a wife and a diamond of a son and could not possibly be allowed to drop such jewels into the empty hand of death. It seemed better to them to choose a middle way, so they gave the Queen a handful of coins to support herself and her child and sent them away never to return.

Poor Penta took her son in her stunted arms

and set off, weeping and wandering. She arrived in a place which was ruled by a magician. When he saw the beautiful maimed maiden who maimed everyone's heart, he wanted to hear the whole story of her misfortunes, right from the beginning when her brother had so appallingly mistreated her. After he had heard everything, the magician could not stop crying. But he gave her a spendid set of rooms in his palace and ordered that she was to be treated as his daughter. Then he issued a proclamation that whoever came to his court and told the most impressive tale of great misfortune would receive a golden crown and sceptre that were worth more than the whole country!

Well, of course, once the proclamation began to spread, more people than there were beetles and caterpillars began to arrive at the magician's palace. One man told how he had worked all his life at a court and had been given only a lump of cheese for his pension. Another man had been kicked in the arse every day for five years by his employer and could do nothing about it. There was a chap who sobbed aloud as he told how his wife was allergic to him and sneezed without stopping if he came near her, so they had no children. Then there was a woman whose nose was so long that dogs chased after her in the street, barking with delight.

Meanwhile, the King had returned home and discovered that everything was heartbreak and bitterness. He was about to have his advisers flogged and skinned when they showed him the letter. When he saw that it was forged, he sent for the captain and heard all about the fisherman's wife on the beach. Realising that she had done all this, he set sail at once and found her himself.

This time, the wife was plied with fine wine by the King and he got the whole story from her, beginning to end. When he learned what she had done to Penta, simply out of jealousy, he ordered that she be made into a candle. So she was waxed and greased and stuck on top of a huge pile of dry wood. The King himself lit the match and when he saw her dance a horrible tango with the hot red fire, he got up and sailed away.

Out on the high seas, he passed another ship carrying the King who was Penta's brother, who told him about the magician's proclamation. The weak brother reckoned that nobody in the world had suffered the misery and bad luck that he had, and was on his way to try for the reward.

'If that's the way of it,' said the King, 'I can beat you with my hands tied behind my back. In fact, I can beat anyone, my agony and misfortune have been so relentlessly awful. Let's agree to compete like gentlemen and whoever wins will share with the other.'

So they shook on it to seal the deal and eventually landed close to the magician's palace. He received them with the honour due to kings. Then he sat them down under a canopy and asked to hear of all their woes.

The brother began by telling how disgracefully he had treated his own sister and how honourably she had behaved in cutting off her hands. He had acted like a dog, locking her in a chest and throwing her to the waves. His conscience was a purgatory of remorse and shame. Even worse, he was grief-stricken by the loss of his good and brave sister. If all the sorrows of the souls in hell were weighed against his, his suffering would be greatest.

When the brother fell silent, the King said, 'Pah! Your pain is nothing compared to my torture.

I found a handless maiden in a trunk and she became my beloved wife. She bore me a gorgeous son, but I had them nearly burned alive because of the trickery of an evil fishwife. They were both exiled from my kingdom and now I can have no peace, day or night, and my blood is like knives is my veins.'

After the magician had listened to the two kings, he realised that one was the brother and the other the husband of Penta. So he called for Penta's son and said, 'Kiss the feet of your father.'

The boy obeyed the magician, and the King his father, seeing how gentle and lovely he was, placed a golden chain around his neck.

Then the magician said, 'Kiss the hand of your uncle.'

The boy did as he was asked, swiftly and gracefully, and the uncle, impressed by the boy's manners, gave him a precious ruby and asked the magician if he was his son.

'Ask the mother,' replied the magician.

Penta, who had been concealed behind a curtain, came out in a state of rapture. She ran back and forth between her brother and her husband, feeling the love of family on the one hand and the love of passion on the other. They made a triangle of joy, talking excitedly and laughing, making a kind of human music. Then they pulled the boy into the magic circle and the father and uncle took turns in throwing him in the air with delight. At the end of all this pure joy, the magician spoke:

'Only heaven will know how happy I am to see Queen Penta comforted at last, because she deserves to be cherished for her wonderful qualities. That is why I started this competition in the hope of bringing her husband and her brother here. I will keep the word of my proclamation and I have decided that the Queen's husband has suffered most. He will receive not only the golden crown and sceptre but also my kingdom here. With your agreement, I would like to be a father and grandfather to you all, and you will be as precious to me as my eyes.'

And since he wanted nothing more than to make Penta happy, the magician told her to put her stumps beneath her apron and to keep them there till he asked her to bring them out, when she would have two warm and living hands.

Penta did as he said and it was true and she held

her child's face in her hands, which were even more beautiful than before.

Then they were all unbelievably happy for ever, because until you've tasted bitterness, you do not know what sweetness is.

Tattercoats

very wealthy old Lord lived in a great palace by the sea. His wife and children were no longer living, but he had one little granddaughter whom he had never set eyes on since the day she was born. He hated her bitterly because his favourite daughter had died giving birth to her. When the nurse brought him the newborn baby, he raged that he would never look at its face as long as it lived and swore that it could live or die as it liked!

He turned his back and sat by his window staring at the ocean and weeping for his lost daughter and would not move. His white hair and beard grew like sorrow over his shoulders, down his back, twining round his chair and creeping across the floor. His great tears dropped onto the windowsill, and wore away the stone, till they ran away, a salty river of grief, into the sea.

Meanwhile, the little granddaughter grew up with no one to love or care for her or even clothe her properly. Only the old nurse, if no one was around, would give her some leftovers from the kitchen or a torn petticoat from the ragbag. But the other palace servants would force her from the house with pokes and pinches and cruel comments. They called her 'Tattercoats' and jeered at her bare feet, till she ran away crying and hid in the garden.

In this way, Tattercoats grew up, with not much to eat or wear, wandering the fields and meadows with not even a pair of shoes. Her only companion was the gooseherd. When she was hungry or cold, he would play to her on his pipe, so merrily that she forgot her troubles. Tattercoats danced to the gooseherd's pipe, with his flock of geese as partners.

One day, the people began to talk excitedly about a splendid ball that the King was giving in the town nearby. The King was travelling the land with his only son, who was to choose a bride and all the lords and ladies of the county were to be invited.

Sure enough, an invitation was delivered to the palace by the sea, and the servants brought it to the old Lord, who still sat by his window, shrouded in his long white hair and weeping into the river that was swollen by his tears.

But when he heard the King's command, he stopped crying and dried his red eyes. He told his servants to fetch shears to cut him loose, because his hair had tied him up like bereavement's prisoner and he could not move. Then he sent them for his finest clothes and most impressive jewels and dressed in them. He ordered them to put the gold saddle on his white horse so that he could ride out splendidly to meet the King.

Tattercoats had heard all about the exciting events in the town. She sat crying by the kitchen door because she could not go. When the old nurse heard the girl's distress, she went to the Lord and pleaded with him to take his granddaughter to the King's ball.

The old Lord scowled and told her to hold her tongue, while the servants roared with laughter and said, 'Tattercoats is happy in her rags, playing with the gooseherd, and that's all she's fit for!'

A second time, and then a third, the nurse begged the Lord to take the girl to the ball. But she only received black looks and dark words, till she was pushed out of the room by the sneering servants.

In tears by now, the old nurse went looking for Tattercoats – but the cook had swept Tattercoats away with a broom and she'd run to the gooseherd to tell him how unhappy she was over the King's ball.

The gooseherd listened, then told her to cheer up. He said that they should go together to the town to see the King and all the wonderful things themselves. When Tattercoats looked sadly down at her torn petticoat and her bare feet, he played on his pipe so entertainingly that she felt better at once. The boy took her by the hand and they danced down the road towards the town, with the geese dancing before them.

They hadn't gone very far, when a handsome young man in the finest clothes rode up and asked the way to the castle where the King was staying. When they said that they were going that way, he dismounted and walked beside them along the road.

The gooseherd began to play a low, sweet tune on his pipe. The stranger gazed and gazed at Tattercoats' beautiful face till he fell deeply in love with her and begged her to marry him.

Tattercoats laughed and shook her lovely head.

'You would be disgraced if your wife was a goosegirl! Ask one of the fine ladies you'll meet at the ball and don't tease poor Tattercoats.'

But the more she declined his proposal, the sweeter the pipe played and the deeper the young man fell in love. To prove his sincerity, he asked her to come at midnight to the King's ball, exactly as she was, with the geese and the gooseherd. He would dance with her – rags, bare feet and all – in front of the King and the noblest in the county; then introduce her as his beloved, beautiful bride.

So when night fell, and the castle ballroom was brilliant with light and music, and the lords and ladies pranced before the King, just as the clock struck twelve, Tattercoats, the gooseherd and his flock of noisy geese came in through the great doors and walked up the ballroom. All around them, the ladies whispered and sniggered and the lords scoffed and guffawed, while the King on his throne stared

in astonishment. But Tattercoats' lover was seated next to the King and he rose to greet her. Taking her by the hand he kissed her passionately, then turned to the King.

'Father,' he said, for it was the Prince himself, 'I have made my choice and here is my bride – the most beautiful girl in all the land, and the kindest too.'

Before he had finished speaking, the gooseherd began to play a melody on his pipe that sounded as sweet as a bird singing in the woods. As he played, Tattercoats' petticoat was changed to a shining gown sewn with glittering jewels. A tiara gleamed in her hair, and the flock of geese behind her became an escort of elegant pages and bridesmaids, holding her long train.

As the King stood to welcome his new daughter, the trumpets played a fanfare in honour of the Princess, and the people outside in the streets told each other that the Prince had chosen for his wife the most beautiful girl in the land, and the kindest too!

The gooseherd was never seen or heard of again, and to this day no one knows what became of him.

The old Lord clopped home to his palace, because he could not stay at court when he had sworn never to look on his granddaughter's face.

He is still sitting by his window, weeping his bitter tears into the river that runs into the sea.

Invisible

his lad lived happily with his parents on the edge of a village in the very last cottage before the forest began.

His mother worked in the woods collecting chestnuts, hazelnuts and walnuts.

His father laboured as a woodcutter, chopping up wood for furniture and fuel.

But one terrible day the father had an accident in the forest and died. The lad and his mother wept as the father was buried in a coffin nailed together from wood he had cut down himself. They grieved for two winters, but when spring came again, the lad's mother met a new man and married him.

When his mother and stepfather came home from their honeymoon, the lad was waiting for them.

His mother ran to him and kissed him, but his stepfather looked straight through him as though he wasn't there.

When bedtime came, the lad kissed his mother goodnight, but when he looked to do the same to his stepfather, the man ignored him and carried on reading his book.

The lad climbed the stairs and lay on his narrow bed. The moon stooped and stared at him through the window with its scarred old face. The lad got up and looked out at the forest where his father had died, where alder, ash, aspen, willow, beech, cherry, poplar, oak, birch, hawthorn, hazel, juniper, lime, rowan, pine, elm and yew whispered in the darkness; but his sorrow had hardened now and his tears were small glass stones in his eyes.

The lad slept late and when he came down for breakfast, his mother had already left to collect nuts in the forest.

His stepfather was writing letters at the table and barely glanced at him when he sat down with his milk and his bread roll.

The lad ate in silence, conscious of the small slurps he made as he drank. The air around his stepfather seemed dark and heavy, as though he made his own weather. He was a handsome man, unsmiling and strong. There were black hairs on the back of his hands. The man looked up and the lad jumped, worried that he'd been caught staring. But the stepfather said nothing, took his coat from the back of the kitchen door and went out, banging the door behind him. The lad went to the mirror on the wall and stared at his pale thin face.

A sunny day came and the lad knew there was to be a trip to the travelling fair that was on in the big town. He woke early and washed himself and brushed his hair and got dressed in his favourite clothes. But when he came downstairs, he saw that his mother had been crying. His stepfather walked past him without a word and went outside to wait for his wife by the gate. The mother couldn't look her son in the eyes.

She pressed some coins into his palm and told him that he wasn't to come to the fair, but was to stay behind and buy himself some lunch from the village shop. They would be back late, she said, and he was to be in bed when they returned.

Her son shouted at her and chucked the coins at her feet, but she shook her head and hurried to the gate to join her husband. The lad left the coins glinting on the floor and promised himself that he would go hungry rather than spend them. He stuffed his pockets with nuts from his mother's collecting basket and ran to the woods.

Dusk came and the forest sulked and darkened. The lad grew cold and climbed down from the branch he'd been sitting on. He made his way back along the path, passing the stumps of trees cut down by his dead father. There was no one at home. He ate some fruit from the bowl, then went up to bed. Hours later, the noise of his mother and stepfather returning to the cottage woke him. His door was ajar and he saw them go past on the way to their bedroom. The lamp on the landing lit up their faces, but they did not look in his room.

The days and weeks and months went on till spring, summer and autumn were gone and it was winter again. The lad moved round the house like a ghost and if ever he caught his mother's eye she looked away. He had stopped going to school, but nobody seemed to notice; and when his stepfather met the schoolteacher in the village inn, nothing was said.

One day, the lad came into the kitchen for an apple and saw his stepfather standing there. The lad reached for the apple in the bowl but as he did so the stepfather's big hand swooped down and seized it. He looked into the man's eyes and heard the crunch as he bit into the apple, but the man strolled past him, brushing against him as though he was air, as though he was nothing.

The lad went to the mirror again, but when he gazed there he could only see the reflection of the kitchen – his mother's empty collecting basket on the table, the man's heavy coat hanging on the hook of the door. He leaned closer to the mirror and breathed, but the glass stayed as bright and clear as before. He pressed the flat palm of his hand against it, but although he could feel the coldness of the mirror he could see nothing of himself.

Terrified, with his heart jerking in his chest, the lad ran upstairs to his mother's bedroom. He sat down at the stool in front of the dressing table and stared wildly into each of the three mirrors there. His face was in none of them.

He fled downstairs and into the sitting room where his mother and stepfather sat. In her arms, his mother held a new baby, carefully wrapped in a soft white blanket. He called his mother's name, but she bent low over the baby's head and made a shushing sound. The stepfather stood up and walked towards him, tall and brooding.

The lad backed away before him and the man shut the door in his face.

And now the lad was truly invisible. He had grown in the year since his mother had married again and his clothes were tight-fitting or too short. Since no one could see him, he put on a big old shirt of his father's and went about in that. He left home in the morning and spent his days in the forest.

In the evenings, he returned to the cottage, taking some food – bread or fruit or nuts – up to his room and eating it there. Sometimes he stood at the side of the baby's crib and looked down at his half-brother, but he was always quiet as he knew the child could not see him.

If he passed his mother in the house, she busied herself at something, or buried her face in her baby's neck. To his stepfather, he was less than a shadow on the stairs. At night he lay alone on his bed, hearing his mother cry and the man shout.

Time passed. One day, as he walked in the woods, the young man, who was tall now and broad-shouldered, saw a girl of his own age sitting on the branch of his favourite tree and swinging her legs. So used was he to being invisible, that he stood and stared at her from the path. But the girl turned her bright hazel eyes on his and laughed at him.

Then she reached into the dense foliage of the tree, rustled there, and tossed him the shiniest, reddest apple in the world. He caught it low with his left hand, like a catch at cricket. Then he remembered that he had on only his father's old shirt, which came to his knees, so he turned and ran away into the forest, clutching the apple. But the girl jumped down from the tree and chased him, and as she was a faster runner than the young man, she soon caught up with him, and she grabbed him by his shirt-tail and kissed him on the lips.

When he woke the next morning, the young man climbed up to the small attic and found the chest which contained his dead father's things.

He put on some soft corduroy trousers, a clean linen shirt and a beautiful leather jacket, which still held the scent of wood shavings and pine. He took out his father's watch, set it to the right time and put it on his wrist. He pulled on warm socks and good boots.

He went downstairs to the kitchen, where his mother was preparing breakfast. She stared at him and tears scalded her eyes and he knew that she saw him. But the girl from the woods was waiting by the gate and he went out to meet her.

He came home late, under the light of stars that had taken years to arrive, and went to his bed. In the morning, he went off with the girl again, and he felt his mother drink him in with her eyes as she watched him go.

After a month and a day of this, he arrived home one night and found his stepfather in the kitchen. The man looked older and smaller now that the young man had grown so tall and fit, and his black hair was greying. He shouted to the young man that he needn't think he could come and go as he pleased, and with a shock the young man realised that the man was looking at him at last. But he pushed his stepfather easily away and went up to his bed. As he lay there, he heard the man's yells and his mother's wails. Outside his window, the moon scudded high up in the clouds, like a coin tossed for heads or tails.

The next day, the son woke early and for the first time made breakfast for his mother and her child and himself. As they were eating, the stepfather came in, but the son didn't glance at him and eventually the man went awkwardly away.

That night, when the young man came home, he brought the girl with him and cooked a meal for them all, so that she could meet his mother and her child.

The stepfather came in again, just as the son was slicing up a pie, but the son ignored him until the man muttered to himself and disappeared.

Every morning, the young man rose early to prepare breakfast and each night he came home with the girl and cooked supper. He worked in the forest now, chopping wood as his father had done.

When the girl looked at him, she had love in her hazel eyes, like a light, and as it shone on him he grew stronger and more handsome.

The mother stared at her two sons and began to notice all the ways in which they were alike. There was no more shouting or crying in the house and the son resolutely treated his stepfather as though he was invisible.

The sullen man kept to himself and bothered nobody. One day he vanished altogether, taking his coat from the hook on the back of the door, and it was as though he had never been there at all. The young man worked hard in the forest to keep food on the table for the family and the girl took the collecting basket from the mother to gather chestnuts, hazelnuts and walnuts.

They were all very happy and as his small half-brother grew, the young man made sure to watch over him, with the light of love in his eyes.

Nine Words

long time ago – before the invention of writing or even sign language – there was a Prince who was put under a curse by a wicked witch. He had done nothing wrong, but her evil spell was that the Prince could only speak one word each year. He was permitted to save up the words, though – so that if he kept shtum for a whole year then the next year he could speak two words, and so on and so forth.

One day he met a beautiful Princess and fell madly in love with her, body and soul. With almost superhuman effort he set out not to speak for two whole years so that he could take her hand, look at her and say, 'My darling.' But at the end of the two years he wanted to tell her that he loved her. So he waited another three long years without uttering a peep. This brought the number of dumb years to five.

At the end of five years, he knew that he just had to ask her to marry him. So he bit his lip and endured another one, two, three, four years in total silence.

At last, as the ninth year of wordlessness ended, he took the lovely Princess to the most private and romantic spot in the royal garden and heaped a hundred red roses into her lap. Then he knelt before her, took her hand, looked into her eyes and croaked out in a hoarse voice:

'My darling! I love you! Will you marry me?'

And the Princess tidied a strand of her soft hair behind the most beautiful of ears, opened her dreamy eyes wide, parted her soft pink lips and said, 'Pardon?'

Wooden Maria

King and his wife had a beautiful only daughter, Maria. When Maria was fifteen, her beloved mother became fatally ill and there was nothing to be done. Maria's father knelt sobbing at the Queen's bedside and vowed that he would never marry again. But his wife hushed him tenderly. 'I must die,' she said. 'But you have our daughter to raise. I am leaving you this ring. You must promise to marry the woman whose finger fits the ring.'

The bleak mourning-time passed and the King began to search for a new wife. He went from one woman to another, but the ring was too big for half of them and too small for the rest. He was secretly relieved and decided to leave things as they were for now.

But one day Maria was rummaging through her mother's things and she found the ring at the back of a drawer. She tried it on and couldn't get it off. 'What will Father say?' she wondered. So she wrapped a bandage round her finger and when her father noticed she said she had cut her finger. He insisted on taking a look, undid the bandage and there was the ring! 'Oh my goodness, Maria!' he exclaimed. 'I will have to marry *you*!'

Maria was shocked and laughed and cried at the same time. 'I can't be your wife! I'm your daughter!'

But the King was adamant he must keep to his promise and Maria went along with it on condition he bring her a dress the colour of meadows and all the flowers in the world; another dress the colour of the sea with every fish in it; and a bridal gown the colour of the sun, the moon and all the stars. She reckoned she was demanding the impossible, but after six months of searching, her father presented her with the three gowns, each one in its own way the most amazing that could be imagined.

'One thing more,' said Maria.

'What else could you possibly wish for?' said her father.

'I want another dress, made of wood.'

The King immediately had a wooden dress made and for the first time in ages, Maria seemed pleased.

On the day of the wedding, she put on the three gorgeous dresses, then the wooden dress on top, and set off for the river. She pretended to bathe, then threw herself in; but instead of sinking and drowning, she floated away, down the river, out to sea, bobbing over the waves, on and on, until she came to a place where a King's son was fishing.

'I've never seen a fish like that,' he thought, and he spread his net and pulled her onto dry land.

'Who are you and where are you from?' he asked.

'I am Wooden Maria and I go where the water takes me.'

'Why are you dressed in wood? Why do you float without drowning?'

She told him that she was a poor girl who had only a wooden dress that floated like a boat, and that she wanted to be of service.

'What can you do?'

'Everything and nothing.'

This amused him so he took her to his castle and

hired her as a rat-catcher for the rats were forever plundering the eggs from the geese. Instead of setting traps for the rats, Maria whistled and sang jolly tunes and tapped out the rhythms on her wooden dress so that soon enough the rats became her pets and danced around her. She fed them on scraps from the kitchen and the rats left the geese and their eggs in peace.

Every evening, Wooden Maria returned to the castle with a basket of eggs and one evening she found the King's son getting ready to go to the ball.

'Where are you off to, heir to the King?'

'Mind your own business, wooden thing!'

'Take me dancing to the ball?'

'You don't have a chance at all!'

Maria grew quiet, but when she was alone she put on the dress the colour of meadows and all the flowers in the world and became the most beautiful woman that was ever seen. At the ball, she sat near the King's son. He asked her at once to dance and would dance with no one else. He fell head over heels in love with her and gave her the gold pin from his lapel.

'Who are you and where are you from?' he asked.

'I am the Countess Thwartscoff,' she replied, but no one there knew her at all. Before the ball was over, she disappeared and the King's son could not find her. She hurried home and put on her wooden dress.

The following evening, he dressed again for the ball and Wooden Maria said to him:

'Your Highness, take me as your guest.'

'Not in that ugly wooden dress!'

'Take me dancing! Please be kind!'

'Silence! I have something on my mind.'

And he grew angry and threatened her with a stick.

After he'd gone, Maria put on the dress the colour of the sea with every fish in it. When she arrived at the ball, the guests gaped because they had never seen someone so beautiful. The men formed a queue to ask her to dance, but she would say yes only to the King's son.

'Who are you and where are you from?' he beseeched.

'I am the Duchess Thwartstick,' was all she would say. The King's son was besotted and gave her the diamond ring from his pinkie. They danced and danced then suddenly she disappeared and the smitten Prince ran everywhere but no one could tell him where she had gone.

The next evening as he prepared for the ball, he was in an agony of hope and despair. Wooden Maria came up to him but he was in no mood for her rat-catcher's cheek and he shoved her away. At the ball, her beauty was dazzling, for she wore the gown the colour of the sun, the moon and all the stars. The King's son gave her the locket from round his neck which held his portrait.

'Who are you and where do you come from?' he begged.

He knelt enraptured at her feet as she told him she was Princess Thwartshove, and the next moment she had given him the slip.

The King's son was struck down with lovesickness and took to his bed. Each day he grew worse, asking everyone over and over if they knew anything about the beautiful girl and swearing he would die unless he saw her again. The whole castle thought he was bonkers. Wooden Maria heard everything and said nothing.

One day, when the King's son was more dead than alive, she slipped something in the soup the son was to sup. Not a soul saw her and the butler took him the soup. He managed a spoonful but something sharp stuck in his throat and he coughed it up. It was the golden pin he had given to the gorgeous Countess!

'Who made this soup?' he gasped.

'The cook made it,' said the butler.

'Well, I can't eat it. Bring me something else immediately.'

The cook was put out and asked the rat-catcher girl to fetch eggs for an omelette. But when he turned his back, she dropped the diamond ring into the mixture. The King's son took a bite of the omelette and nearly broke a tooth on the diamond. Then he ordered that Wooden Maria was to make him a pie. The cook, the butler and the rest of the staff complained about this loopy behaviour, but the pie was made and dished up soon enough. When the pining Prince forked out the locket with his portrait, he ran down to the yard.

There he found the rats dancing around the girl in the wooden dress, singing:

'She dresses in wood
And loves who she should!'

Then Maria told him her story from beginning to end and before anyone knew it they were hand in glove and deep in love and wife and man and King and Queen, through tears and laughter, happy ever after.

The Squire's Bride

big old Squire owned a dirty great manor and had loads of gold stashed in his chest and plenty more coming in from money-lending. But something was missing, because he was a widower. The young lass from the nearby farm worked for him and he'd taken a right shine to her. Her family was hard up and he reckoned that if he so much as hinted or winked at matrimony she'd be all over him like a rash. So he told her that he had hit upon the notion of getting wed again.

'Ooh! It's surprising what one can hit upon!' said the girl, standing there giggling. She reckoned the revolting old goat should've hit upon something else!

'Well, I have hit upon the idea that *you* should be

my new wife!' said the Squire.

The young girl replied prettily, 'Thanks, but no thanks!' and thought, 'That day will be a long time coming, Squire!'

Of course, the less she wanted him, the more he wanted her and he wasn't used to taking 'in your dreams' for an answer. He got nowhere with the lass, so he sent for her father. If the father could fix him up with the girl, he could forget about the money he owed him and the Squire would throw in that piece of land next to his field on top.

The father thought his daughter was only a child who didn't know what was best for her. Yes, he promised the Squire, he'd sort it, no problem.

But his daughter would have none of it, whether he yelled or wheedled. She wouldn't marry the Squire if he sat in powdered gold from arsehole to earhole, so there!

The Squire waited for news, day and night, but no, nowt. At last, angry and impatient, he told the father he couldn't wait any longer. If the father was to keep his promise, he must settle matters at once.

The father told the Squire to get everything ready for the wedding and when the parson and all the guests were assembled, he was to send for the girl on a work pretext. When she arrived, she must be spliced in a trice, before she knew what was to do.

'Good plan, good plan,' said the smitten Squire. So he had his servants brew and bake like maniacs, had a wedding cake made and a wedding punch concocted. And when everyone arrived in their finery for the feast the Squire told one of his lads to run down to the farm and have the father send up what he'd promised. He shook his fist at the lad and told him to be back in the pop of a cork or he'd get what for, so the lad legged it.

'I've come from the Squire to fetch what you promised him,' he said to the father. 'But it has to be this instant because he's in a right old state today.'

'No problem! No problem! Get down to the field and take her with you. You'll see her there.'

The boy rushed to the field and saw the daughter raking there. 'I'm to take what your father promised the Squire,' he said.

The girl wasn't daft. 'Is that right?' she said. 'It's the little white mare over there by the cabbages. Take her away.'

The lad jumped onto the little mare's back and

galloped home at full pelt.

'Did you get her?' asked the Squire.

'She's standing by the front door,' replied the lad.

'Well, take her up to Mother's bedroom!' said the Squire.

'Bloody hell! How's that to be managed?' said the lad.

The Squire thought he meant the girl might kick up a fuss. 'Do as I say,' he said, 'and if you can't manage her on your own, get the others to help you.'

The Squire was scarlet in the face, so the lad got all the servants together and some hauled on the front half and some shoved on the back, and at last they got the mare up the stairs and into the bedroom. The wedding dress, veil, gloves and so on were all laid out for the Squire's bride.

'I've taken her upstairs, Squire,' said the lad. 'But it was the worst job I've had since I started work here.'

'It'll be worth it,' said the Squire. 'Now send some women up to dress her.'

'Bloody hell! How's that to be done?' said the lad.

'None of your lip! They're to get her dressed and to forget neither garter nor garland,' snapped the Squire.

The lad went to the kitchen. 'Listen, girls,' he said, 'get yourselves upstairs and dress that little mare as a bride. The Squire must want to give his guests a good laugh.'

So the housemaids put the bridal outfit on the mare and the lad went to the Squire to tell him she was ready, and wearing both garter and garland.

'Tickety-boo!' said the Squire. 'Bring her down and I'll greet her at the door myself.'

There was an almighty clattering on the stairs and the sound of snorting and neighing. Then the door opened, the Squire's bride came into the great hall, and all the wedding guests fell about laughing.

And it must have been a very happy union, because they reckon the Squire hasn't gone courting since!

The Lost Happy Endings

he Rat's job was important. Each evening when dusk was removing the outlines of things, like a rubber, the Rat had to shoulder his sack and carry all the Happy Endings of stories from one end of the forest to the other, in time for everybody's bedtime. Then the Rat had to climb onto the branch of the ancient oak tree, open the sack and shake out the Happy Endings into the darkening air.

Some of the Endings drifted away like breath and others fluttered upwards like moths fumbling for light. Some looked like fireflies disappearing among the kindling of the leaves and twigs and some were fireworks, zipping skywards like rockets and flouncing off in a jackpot of sparks high above the forest.

When the last Ending was out of the sack, the Rat would scamper and rustle his way homewards through the woods. Sometimes the eyes of owls flashed from the trees like torches and made him jump, or bats skimmed the top of his head like living frisbees and he squeaked with surprise; but the Rat ran speedily along and was soon home in his hole.

He would sleep quite late the following day. By the time he'd washed, eaten and visited other rats down by the river, the Happy Endings had flown back to the forest like homing pigeons and were hanging from the old silver birch all ready for the Rat to collect once more.

One evening, as the Rat set off with his sack, he noticed scarves of mist draped in the trees. One of them noosed itself round the Rat's neck, soft and damp, and made him shiver.

By the time he had reached the middle of the forest, the mist had thickened and the Rat could only see a little way ahead. The shadowy trees looked villainous: tall ghouls with long arms and twiggy fingers. Bushes crouched in the fog as though they might pounce like muggers. The Rat hurried on.

'Hello, my verminous deario!'

The Rat jumped. A twisted old witch with a face like the bark of a tree and horrible claw hands was standing on the path in front of the Rat. She had fierce red eyes like poisonous berries.

'What's in the sack?'

'Let me pass,' said the Rat.

'What's in the sack, I said!'

The witch had grabbed hold of the Rat's tail. Her touch nipped like pepper.

'Let me alone!' gasped the Rat. 'I must go on.'

'Shut up, rodent!' said the vicious witch, and she spat green spittle in the Rat's face. The Rat was so shocked that he jumped backwards and rolled over a tree root. Faster than fury, the witch was on him and had snatched the sack of Happy Endings.

'I'm having this, my rat-faced deario,' she snarled. Then she gobbed at the Rat again and hobbled rapidly away into the darkness and the fog. The Rat cowered for a long time, terrified that the witch would return.

The fog began to lift and the moon turned the narrow path through the forest to a long silver finger. An owl's hoot questioned sadly. The Rat looked about. The Happy Endings were lost! He turned and ran back down the path to his home, scattering bitter tears into the cold black night.

As the Rat ran crying through the forest, children in their beds were listening to their bedtime stories. But tonight there were to be no Happy Endings.

Wooden Maria sank to the bottom of the sea and she drowned. The children started to cry.

The lass who worked on the farm was forced to marry the old squire and scrub him in the bath before bed. The children started to scream.

The children of Hamelin, trapped inside the

mountain, ate each other or starved to death. The children had hysterics.

On and on the parents of the children read, and worse and worse the tales became. Soon the night was filled with the awful sound of frightened and traumatised children weeping and wailing in their beds.

There was a cacophony of children crying or asking for the light to be left on or refusing to sleep alone or wetting the bed. The Rat rocked back and forth moaning with sorrow.

When dawn came, it grew quieter, and the exhausted Rat fell fast asleep. As he slept, he dreamed of a Golden Pen, which could write on night itself . . .

He seized the pen and set off into the forest. It grew dark. Stars whispered.

The Rat dreamed that he came to the spot where the witch had snitched his sack.

Wondering what to do, he held the Golden Pen and drew a question mark on the night air. It floated before him, glowing in the darkness.

Suddenly the Rat knew exactly what to do. He would write his own Happy Ending on the night! He wrote in the air and every word shone out in perfect golden handwriting:

'When the witch first opened the sack of Happy Endings she was furious. They were worthless to a witch. Boring. Stupid.

'She flung the sack into the corner of her lair and went out to bite the head off any small songbird she could catch and crunch its beak. It was good to be bad. Then she decided to burn the sack of Happy Endings. She would dance around the fire and shout out terrible swear words and drink poison-berry juice and smoke a clay pipe. Good to be bad.

'So she lugged the sack outside, added a few dried leaves and twigs, then squatted down and began to rub two sticks together to light the fire.

'The rapid movement of her witchy hands made a spark, then another, and another, and soon the fire was born. Suddenly a spark leapt from the stick and jumped onto a lock of her frizzy old hair. There was a nasty burny hairy smell and – *whumph!* The Witch's hair was alight.

'She shrieked horribly, beating at her head with her hands. She danced crazily around the fire, singing hideously. The flames danced with her, cheek to cheek, step by step, arm in arm, one-two-three, one-two-three. Her screams scattered the sleeping birds from the trees in a panic of wings.'

The Rat heard an awful noise and smelled something strange cooking. He followed his nose and it led him to the bowels of the forest. The fire opened its jaws and roared.

He stared in horror into the Witch's small red eyes until they were burned completely black and the Witch collapsed in a sullen hiss of ash . . .

He saw the sack on the ground.

The sack of Happy Endings!

There was still time, if he ran as fast as he ever had in his life, to send the Happy Endings out into the world.

Goosegirls went to the ball and grooms lived happily ever after . . .

Squires with little taste and loads of cash produced as much food as a peasant could ever wish for and . . . Look! Look! Look! Lost children were running home through the woods into the arms of their parents.

Hansel and Gretel

t was no more than once upon a time when a poor woodcutter lived in a small house at the edge of a huge, dark forest. Now, the woodcutter lived with his wife and his two young children – a boy called Hansel and a little girl called Gretel. It was hard enough for him to feed them all at the best of times – but these were the worst of times; times of famine and hunger and starvation; and the woodcutter was lucky if he could get his hands on even a simple loaf of bread. Night after hungry night, he lay in his bed next to his thin wife, and he worried so much that he tossed and he turned and he sighed and he mumbled and moaned and he just couldn't sleep at all. 'Wife, wife, wife,' he said to Hansel's and Gretel's stepmother. 'What

are we going to do? How can we feed our two poor children when we've hardly enough for ourselves? Wife, wife, what can be done?' And as he fretted and sweated in the darkness, back came the bony voice of his wife – a voice as fierce as a famine. 'Listen to me, husband,' she said. 'Tomorrow at first light we'll take the children into the forest, right into the cold, black heart of it. We'll make a fire for them there and give them each one last morsel of bread. Then we'll pretend to go off to our work and we'll leave them there all by themselves. They'll never be able to find their way back home on their own. We'll be rid of them for good and only have to worry about feeding ourselves.' But when the woodcutter heard these hard, desperate words he said no. 'No, no, wife, I can't do that. How could I have the heart to leave young Hansel and Gretel in the forest? The wild beasts would soon sniff them out and eat them alive.' But his wife was adamant. 'You fool,' she said with tight lips, 'do you want all four of us to starve to death? You might as well start smoothing the wood for our coffins.' And she gave the poor, heartsore woodcutter no peace until he agreed to do as she said. 'But I feel so sorry for my helpless little children,' he wept. 'I can't help it.'

Now, Hansel and Gretel had been so hungry that night that they hadn't been able to sleep either, and they'd heard every cruel word of their stepmother's terrible plan. Gretel cried bitter, salt tears, and said to Hansel, 'Now we're finished.' But Hansel comforted her. 'Don't cry, Gretel. Don't be sad. I'll think of a way to save us.' And when their father and stepmother had finally gone to sleep, Hansel got up, put on his coat, opened the back door, and crept out into the midnight hour. There was bright, sparkling moonlight outside and the white pebbles on the ground shone like silver coins and precious jewels. Hansel bent down and filled his empty pockets with as many pebbles as he could carry. Then he went back inside and said to Gretel, 'Don't worry, Gretel, you can go to sleep now. We'll be fine, I promise.' And he got back into bed.

At dawn, before the sun had properly risen, their stepmother came and woke the two children. 'Get up, you lazy scraps, we're going into the forest to chop wood.' Then she gave each of them a miserable mouthful of bread. 'There's your lunch – think yourselves lucky, and don't eat it all at once, because there's nothing else.' Gretel put the bread in her apron pocket, because Hansel's pockets were crammed with pebbles. Then the whole family set off along the path to the forest. Hansel kept stopping and looking back towards the house, until finally the woodcutter called to him, 'Hansel, what are you trailing behind for and looking at? Keep up with the rest of us.' 'Sorry, Father,' said Hansel, 'I'm just looking back at my white kitten. It's sitting up there on our roof, saying goodbye.' 'You stupid boy,' said his stepmother. 'That's not your kitten. It's just the light of the morning sun glinting on the chimney. Now come on.' But, of course, Hansel hadn't been looking at anything at all. He'd been throwing the white pebbles from his pocket onto the path.

The forest was immense and gloomy. When they had reached the middle, the woodcutter said, 'Now, Hansel, now, Gretel, gather up some wood and I'll make a nice fire to keep you warm.' Hansel and Gretel collected a big pile of firewood and when it was set alight and the flames were like burning tongues, their stepmother said, 'Now lie down by the fire and rest. We're going further into the forest to chop wood. When we're finished working, we'll come back and get you.' The children sat by the fire, and when midday came, they chewed on their small portions of bread. They could hear the blows of a woodcutter's axe nearby and they thought that their father was close. But it wasn't an axe, it was just a branch that he had tied to an old, withered tree and the wind was blowing it to and fro, to and fro. After they had waited and waited and waited, the children's eyes grew as heavy as worry and they fell fast asleep.

When at last they woke up, it was already pitch dark, darker than a nightmare. Gretel began to cry and said, 'How are we going to find our way out of this enormous forest?' But Hansel tried to cheer her up. 'Just wait a bit till the moon rises, Gretel, then we'll find our way home all right.' And when the moon had risen, casting its brilliant, magical light, Hansel took his little sister by the hand and followed the pebbles. They shone like newly minted coins, like cats' eyes, like diamonds, and showed them the way. They walked all through the night, and at daybreak they knocked on the door of their father's house. When their stepmother opened it and saw it was Hansel and Gretel, she said, 'You naughty children! Why did you sleep so long in the forest? We thought you were never coming home.' But their father was pleased to have them back again, for he had been grief-stricken at leaving them all by themselves in the forest.

Not long afterwards, times became very hard again and the famine bit deeply and savagely into their lives. One night, when they all lay in bed with gnawing stomachs, the children heard their stepmother's ravenous voice again, 'There's no more food left except half a loaf of bread, and when that's gone that'll be the end of all of us. The children must go, I tell you. Tomorrow first thing, we'll take them even deeper, deeper, right into the belly of the forest so they won't possibly be able to find their way out. It's our only way of saving ourselves.' Although the woodcutter grew very upset and thought that it was better to share your last crumb with your children, his wife wouldn't listen to a word he said. Her sharp voice pecked on and on at him, 'You did it before so you'll do it again. You did it before so you'll do it again.' And in the end, the poor starving woodcutter gave in.

Once more, Hansel waited till his parents fell asleep, and then he got up and tried to get out to collect his pebbles like the last time. But the stepmother had locked and bolted the door and Hansel couldn't get out, no matter how hard he tried. He had to go back to bed empty-handed and comfort his little sister. 'No more tears, Gretel,' he said. 'Just try to sleep. I know somehow I'll find something to help us.'

It was very, very early when their stepmother came and poked the children out of bed. She gave them each a piece of bread, but they were even smaller pieces than before. On the way to the forest, Hansel crumbled his bit of bread in his pocket, and kept pausing to throw a crumb on the ground. 'Hansel, why do you keep stopping and looking behind you?' said the woodcutter. 'Get a move on.' 'I'm only looking back at my little dove, Father,' said Hansel. 'It's sitting on our roof trying to say goodbye to me.' 'You idiotic boy,' snapped his stepmother, 'that isn't your dove. It's the sun shining on the chimneypot.' But carefully, one tiny crumb at a time, Hansel laid a lifeline of bread on the path.

And now the stepmother had led the children right into the deepest, densest part of the forest, to where they had never been in their whole lives. A big, licking fire was lit again and she told them, 'You two sit here and wait, and if you get tired you can go to sleep. Your father and I are going further off to chop wood. And in the evening when we're finished, we'll come and fetch you.'

After a while, Gretel shared her miserly lump of bread with Hansel, who had scattered his piece on the path. Then they fell asleep, and the long evening passed, but nobody came to take them home. The night grew darker and darker, and when they woke up, it was too black to see a thing. 'Don't worry, Gretel,' said Hansel. 'When the moon rises, we'll see the breadcrumbs I dropped. They'll show us our way.' As soon as the full moon came, glowing and luminous, the two children set off.

But they didn't find a single breadcrumb, because all the thousands of birds that fly about in the forest had pecked them away and eaten them. Hansel said to Gretel, 'Don't panic, we'll find our way anyway.' But they didn't find it. They walked all night and all the following day, and by the next evening they were still hopelessly lost in the bowels of the forest. What's worse, they were hungrier than they had ever been in their skinny young lives, because they had nothing to eat except for a few berries they'd managed to scavenge. Eventually, Hansel and Gretel

were so weak and exhausted that their legs wouldn't carry them one step further. So they lay down under a tree and fell fast asleep.

It was now the third morning since they had left their father. The famished, thirsty children forced themselves to walk again, but they only wandered further and further into the forest, and they knew that unless they found help very soon they would die of hunger. When it was midday, they saw a beautiful white bird singing on a branch, and the bird's song was so enchanting that Hansel and Gretel stopped to listen to it. As soon as its song was over, the bird flapped its creamy wings and flew off in front of them, and they followed it till it landed on the roof of a little house. When Hansel and Gretel got closer, they saw that the house had bread walls and a roof made of cake and windows made of clear bright sugar. 'Look!' cried Hansel. 'This will do us! What wonderful luck! I'll try a slice of the roof, Gretel, and you can start on a window. I bet it'll taste scrumptiously sweet.' Hansel stretched up and broke off a bit of the roof to see what it tasted like, and Gretel snapped off a piece of window-pane and nibbled away. Suddenly, they heard a thin little voice calling from inside:

'Stop your nibbling, little rat,
It's my house you're gnawing at.'

But the chomping children chanted:

'We're only the wind going past,
Gently blowing on roof and glass.'

And they just went on munching away. Hansel thought the roof was absolutely delicious and pulled off a great slab of it. Gretel bashed out a whole round window-pane and sat down and had a wonderful chewy time. Then suddenly, the door opened and an old, old woman, bent double on a crutch, came creeping out. Hansel was so scared and Gretel was so frightened that they both dropped what they were holding. But the old woman wagged her wizened head and said, 'Well, well, you sweet little things, how did you get here? Come in and stay with me. You'll come to no harm.' She took the children by the hand and led them into the tempting house. Then she gave them a wonderful meal of creamy milk and mouth-watering pancakes with sugar and chocolate and apples and nuts. After

Hansel and Gretel had eaten as much as they could, she made up two soft, comfy little beds with the best white linen, and Hansel and Gretel lay down to sleep.

But the old crone was only pretending to be kind, for she was really a cruel and evil witch who lay in wait for children and had only built her bread house with its cake roof to trap them. When a child fell into her power, she would kill it, cook it and eat it, and that was her favourite banquet. Witches have red eyes which they can't see very far with – but they have a powerful sense of smell, as good as any animal's, and they can sniff when anyone comes near them. So as Hansel and Gretel had approached her little house in the woods, she'd cackled a spiteful laugh and said nastily, 'Here's two for my belly who shan't escape.'

Early next morning before the children had woken, she was already drooling by their beds, looking greedily down at them. They looked so sweet lying there with their rosy cheeks that she slavered to herself, 'This will make a tasty scram for me to swallow.' Then she seized Hansel with her long claws and dragged him off to a mean shed outside and locked him up behind the door with iron bars. Hansel screamed his head off, but it was no use. Then the witch went to Gretel and jabbed her awake and shouted, 'Get up, you lazy slut, get water and cook a good meal for your brother. He's locked up outside in the shed and I want him fattened up. When he's nice and plump, I'm going to eat him.' Gretel started to cry hot, stinging tears, but it was hopeless, and she had to do what the wicked witch told her.

Day after day, the best meals were cooked for Hansel, while poor Gretel had to survive on crabshells. Every morning, the horrible witch groped and fumbled her way out to the shed and shrieked, 'Hansel, stick out your finger for me to feel if you're plump.' But clever Hansel held out a little bone instead, and the old crone's red witchy eyes couldn't see it. She thought it was Hansel's finger and was furious and surprised that he went on and on not getting plump. After four weeks of this, she lost her patience completely and refused to wait a day longer. 'Now then, Gretel,' she shouted. 'Jump to it and cook him one last meal. Tomorrow, whether he's plump or skinny, fat or thin, I'm going to cut Hansel's throat with my sharpest knife and cook him.' Gretel sobbed and wailed as the witch forced her to carry the water for cooking, and her face was basted with tears. 'Who can help us now?' she cried. 'If only the wild beasts had eaten us in the forest, then at least we'd have died together.' 'You can cut that bawling out,' said the witch. 'It won't do you any good.'

Next morning, Gretel had to go out and hang up a big cooking pot of water and light the fire. 'First we'll bake some bread,' said the witch. 'I've already heated the oven and kneaded the dough.' She pushed and pinched poor Gretel over to where the oven was, with greedy flames leaping out of it already. 'Crawl inside and tell me if it's hot enough for the bread to go in.' And the witch's gruesome, gluttonous plan was to shut the oven door once Gretel was inside, so she could roast her and eat her too. But Gretel guessed this, and said, 'I don't know how to do it. How can I get inside there?' 'You foolish goose,' snapped the witch. 'The opening's big enough for you. I could get into it myself. Look.' And the witch hobbled up and poked her ugly head inside the oven. Then Gretel gave her such a push, such a big shove, that she fell right into the middle of the oven. Gretel slammed the iron door shut with shaking hands and bolted it. The witch began to shriek and howl in the most frightful way; but Gretel ran outside and the heartless witch burned agonizingly to death.

Gretel ran straight to Hansel's shed and opened it, shouting, 'Hansel, we're saved! We're saved! The old witch is dead.' And Hansel jumped out, free as a bird released from a cage, and they both danced and cheered and hugged and kissed. There was nothing to be afraid of any more, so they went into the witch's house and opened all her cupboards, which were stuffed to bursting with pearls and precious stones. 'These are much better than pebbles,' said Hansel. He crammed his pockets with as much as he could, and Gretel said, 'I'll take some home too,' and filled her apron full to the brim. 'Right,' said Hansel. 'Now let's go and get out of this witchy forest for good.'

When the children had walked for a while, they came to the edge of a big, wide river. 'I can't see a bridge anywhere,' said Hansel. 'We won't be able to get across.' 'And there's no boat either,' said Gretel. 'But look! There's a white duck swimming along.

I'm sure it'll help us across if I ask it nicely.' So she called out:

> '*Excuse me, little white duck,*
> *Gretel and Hansel seem to be stuck.*
> *A bridge or a boat is what we lack,*
> *Will you carry us over on your back?*'

Sure enough, the duck came swimming and quacking towards them, and Hansel jumped quickly onto its back and told Gretel to sit behind him. But sensible Gretel said, 'No. That'll be too heavy for the duck. I think it should take us across one at a time.' And that is exactly what the kind little duck did. So Hansel and Gretel walked happily on, and the wood became more and more familiar, until at last they saw their father's house in the distance. They began to run, run, run, charged into the kitchen and flung their arms around their father's neck. The sad, lonely man had not had one happy moment since he had abandoned the children in the forest, and his wife had died and was buried. But Gretel shook out the contents of her apron, making the precious stones twinkle and shine upon the floor, and young Hansel threw down handful after handful of white pearls from his pockets. Now it was certain that all their troubles were over, and the grateful woodcutter and Hansel and Gretel lived on together at the edge of the forest and were happy ever after.

So that was that. Look! There goes a rat! Who'll catch it and skin it and make a new hat?

The Golden Goose

nce there was a man who had three sons. Everyone thought that the youngest son was a simpleton. They called him Dummling, and picked on him, sneered at him, and teased him at every opportunity. One day, the eldest of the three decided to go into the forest and chop wood there. Before he set off, his mother gave him a beautiful, sweet home-made cake and an excellent bottle of wine, in case he needed to eat or drink. When the eldest son entered the forest, he saw a little grey-haired old man who called out good day to him and said, 'Please give me a piece of that cake in your pocket, and let me have a gulp of your good wine. I am so hungry and thirsty.' But the clever son replied coolly, 'Certainly not. If I give you my cake and wine,

I'll have none left for myself and that wouldn't be very smart, would it? Get lost!' And he turned his back on the little man and strode smartly on. But when he began to chop at his first tree, it was only a few moments before he made a stupid stroke with the axe, and cut himself painfully in the arm. So he had to stagger home and have it bandaged. And it was the little grey man who had made this happen.

Soon after that, the second son decided to go to the forest; and he, too, received from his mother a delicious cake and a bottle of the best wine. The little old grey man met him as well, and asked him for a slice of cake and a swig of wine. But the sensible son refused. 'That's out of the question. Anything I give to you means less for me and where's the sense in that? On your way.' And he left the old man standing there and walked on purposefully. But his punishment came quickly; and as he was hacking away at the tree, he cut himself in the leg so deeply that he had to be carried home.

Then Dummling said, 'Father, please let me go and cut wood in the forest.' His father sighed and tutted, 'Your brothers have hurt themselves already doing that. Be quiet, Dummling. You don't know what you're talking about.' But Dummling begged and pleaded for so long that eventually his father said, 'All right then, go! And when you've damaged yourself, perhaps that'll be a lesson to you.' Dummling's mother gave him a tasteless cake made with water and baked in the ashes and a bottle of sour beer to wash it down with. When he arrived in the forest, the little old grey man came up to him and greeted him, 'Give me a bit of your cake and a swallow from your bottle. I am very hungry and thirsty.' Dummling answered simply and honestly, 'I've only got a flour-and-water cake and some stale ale; but if that's good enough for you, you're welcome to share it with me.' So they sat down together, and when Dummling took out his cinder-cake it was now a superb sweet cake, and his sour beer had turned into the finest wine. They ate and drank contentedly, and afterwards the little grey man said, 'Since you have such a kind heart, and share what little you have so generously, I am going to give you the gift of good luck. See that old tree over there? Well, chop it down and you will find something at its roots.' Then the little man left Dummling alone. Dummling went straight over to the tree and cut it down, and when it fell there was a goose sitting in the roots with feathers of pure gold. He lifted her out, tucked her firmly under his arm, and set off for an inn where he intended to stay the night.

Now, the landlord of the inn had three daughters,

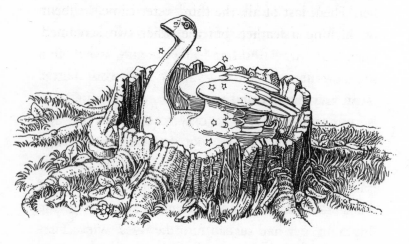

and as soon as they saw the goose they were fascinated by it, and curious to find out what wonderful kind of bird it was. And they ended up by longing for one of its golden feathers. The eldest thought, 'I'll be smart and wait for a good opportunity and then I'll pull out one of its feathers for myself.' And as soon as Dummling had gone out, she grabbed the goose by its wing. But her fingers and hand stuck to the goose like glue. Soon afterwards, the second sister came along with exactly the same cunning idea of plucking out a golden feather all for herself. But no sooner had she touched her older sister than she was stuck to her. Then, last of all, the third sister came, hellbent on filching a feather, but the other two screamed out, 'Stay away! For heaven's sake stay away!' But she didn't see why she should be the only one to keep away, and thought, 'If they're doing it, why shouldn't I?' and rushed over to them. Of course, the moment she'd touched her sister she was stuck to her. And there the three of them had to stay all night, glued to the golden goose.

The next morning, Dummling tucked the goose under his arm and set off into the world, without so much as blinking an eye at the three sisters who were stuck behind him. The silly girls had to run after him, any old way he chose to go – left, right, fast, slow, wherever his legs carried him. As they were crossing the fields, the Parson noticed them, and when he saw the procession following Dummling, he said sternly, 'You ought to be ashamed of yourselves, you disgraceful girls, chasing after a young man through the fields like this. What are young girls coming to?' And at the same time, he seized the youngest by the hand and tried to pull her away. But as soon as his hand touched hers he was stuck fast too, and had to run after them himself till he was puce in the face. Next thing, the Sexton came that way, and seeing the highly respectable Parson, that pillar of the community, running after three girls, he was very shocked indeed and called out, 'Hoy, your reverence, where are you rushing off to? Have you forgotten we've got a christening today?' He trotted up to him and tugged at his sleeve, but was stuck to it at once. While the five of them were jogging like this, one behind the other, two workers from the fields went past with their hoes. The Parson shouted out to them and begged for their help in setting him and the Sexton free. But no sooner had they touched the Sexton than the two of them became firmly stuck, and now there were seven of them running behind Dummling and his golden goose.

Eventually, they all arrived at a city. The King who ruled there had a daughter who was so serious that nothing and no one could make her laugh. Because of this, the King had given his word that whoever could make her laugh could marry her – simple as that. When Dummling heard about this, he went directly to the King's daughter with his goose and the train of seven people behind him. The solemn-faced girl took one look at them all, running up and down as Dummling pleased, and burst out laughing. And she laughed so much it seemed she'd never stop! Straight away, Dummling asked to marry her, as was his right, and soon enough the peals of laughter became peals of wedding bells. The wedding was held at once; and Dummling became heir to the kingdom and lived long and merrily with his wife.

Ashputtel

O ne bleak time, there was a wealthy man whose wife became fatally ill. When she felt that the end of her life was near, she called her only little daughter to her bedside and said, 'My darling girl, always try to be good, like you are now, and say your prayers. Then God will look after you, and I will look down at you from heaven and protect you.' When she'd said these words, she closed her loving eyes and died. The young girl went out every day to cry beside her mother's grave. When winter came, the snow put down a white shroud on the grave, and when the sun took it off again in the spring, the girl's father remarried.

His new wife brought her two daughters to live with them. Although their faces were as lovely as flowers, their hearts were as ugly as thorns. And so, a time of real unhappiness began for the poor little stepdaughter. 'Why should this eyesore sit next to us at supper?' they squawked. 'Those who want to eat bread must earn it. Go to the kitchen, kitchen maid!' They stole her pretty dresses and made her wear an old grey smock and forced her perfect feet into wooden clogs. 'Ooh, la-di-da!' they sniggered. 'Doesn't the proud princess look perfect today!' Their bright, mean eyes gleamed, and they laughed at her and put her in the kitchen. She had to do all the hard work from dawn till dusk – get up before sunrise, fetch water, make the fire and do the cooking and washing. As well as this, her stepsisters bullied her and poured peas and lentils into the ashes, then forced her to sit there and pick them all out. At night, when she was completely worn out and exhausted with work, she was given no bed to sleep in like the others, but had to lie down on the ashes by the hearth. And because this covered her in dust and grime and made her look dirty, they called her 'Ashputtel'.

One day, their father was about to set off to the market fair and he asked his two stepdaughters what they would like as a present. 'Beautiful dresses,' said one. 'Pearls and sparkling diamonds,' said the second. 'But what about you, Ashputtel?' he said. 'What would you like to have?' 'Father, break off the first twig that brushes against your hat on the way home and bring it to me.' So he purchased fine dresses and precious stones for the two stepsisters; and on his way home, as he was riding through a wood, a hazel twig brushed his head and knocked off his hat. So he snapped off the twig and put it in his pocket. As soon as he arrived back home, he gave his stepdaughters what they had asked for – how their eyes widened! – and to Ashputtel he gave the twig from the hazel bush. Ashputtel said thank you, went out to her mother's grave and planted the twig on it. She was so unhappy and cried so much that her tears watered the twig as they fell, and it grew into a beautiful tree. Three times every day Ashputtel went to the tree and wept and said her prayers. Each time, a little white bird came and perched on the tree; and whenever Ashputtel wished for something, the bird would drop whatever it was at her feet.

Now, it happened that the King decided that his son must choose a bride; so he announced that a feast would be held. It was to last for three whole days and all the pretty young girls in the country were to be invited. When the two stepsisters heard that this included them, they were thrilled, and their eyes shone and their feet tapped with excitement. They called Ashputtel and said, 'Comb our hair, brush and polish our shoes and rouge our cheeks. We're going to the wedding feast at the royal palace.' Ashputtel did as they ordered, but she cried because she wanted to go to the dance as well. She begged her stepmother to let her go, but her stepmother sneered, 'You kitchen tramp! Look at yourself. Do you want to go to the feast all dusty and grimy? You haven't any dresses or shoes, so how do you think you can go dancing, you little scruff?' But when Ashputtel kept pleading and pleading, she finally said, 'See here. I've poured this bowl of lentils into the ashes. If you can pick out all the lentils again in two hours, then you can come with us to the dance.'

Ashputtel went through the back door into the garden and called out, 'Gentle doves and turtle-doves, all you birds of the sky come and help me sort out my lentils:

Into the pot if they're nice to eat,
But swallow the bad ones with your beak.'

Then two white doves flew in at the kitchen window, and after them came the turtle-doves, and then all the birds of the air came swooping and crowding in and landed on the floor round the ashes. The doves nodded their small heads and began – peck, peck, pick, pick – and then the other birds joined in – pick, pick, pick, peck, peck, peck – and put all the good lentils into the bowl. They were so quick and efficient that they'd finished within an hour and flown back out of the window. Ashputtel hurried to show the bowl to her stepmother, bursting with happiness at the thought of going to the wedding feast. But her stepmother said, 'No, Ashputtel, you've got no dress and you can't dance. You'll only show us up.' But when Ashputtel burst into tears, she said, 'If you can sort out two bowlfuls of lentils out of the ashes in one hour, you can come with us. She'll never manage that,' thought the stepmother to herself as she poured two bowlfuls of lentils into the ashes. 'It's impossible.'

Ashputtel went out into the garden and called, 'Gentle doves and turtle-doves, all you birds of the sky, come and help me sort my lentils:

Into the pot if they're nice to eat
But swallow the bad ones with your beak.'

Once again, the white doves, then the turtle-doves, then all the many birds of the sky came skimming and swirling in and peck-peck-pecked all the good grains into the bowls. And this time, it wasn't even half an hour before they'd finished and flown out of the window. Ashputtel took the bowls straight to her stepmother, overjoyed at the thought of going to the feast. But her stepmother snapped, 'It's no good. You can't come because you haven't any fine dresses, you haven't any shoes, you can't dance and we'd all be ashamed of you.' And she turned her back on Ashputtel and swept off with her two cruel daughters.

When everybody had gone and the house was empty, Ashputtel went to her mother's grave under the hazel tree and called out:

'Shake your leaves and branches, little tree,
Shower gold and silver down on me.'

And the white bird threw down a golden and silver dress and a pair of slippers embroidered in silk and silver. Quick as a smile, Ashputtel put it all on and hurried to the feast. She looked so stunning in the golden dress that her stepsisters and stepmother couldn't see that it was Ashputtel and thought she must be a Princess from a foreign land. Ashputtel, they thought, even as they stared at this gorgeous girl, was crouched at home in the dirt, squinting and picking lentils out of the ashes. The Prince came over to her, bowed deeply, took her hand and danced off with her. He wouldn't let go of her hand, or dance with anyone else, and if another man came up and asked her to dance, he said, 'She is my partner.'

Ashputtel danced till it was evening, and then she wanted to go home. But, because the Prince was desperate to find out whose beautiful daughter this was, he announced, 'I shall come with you and escort you home.' But Ashputtel managed to slip away from him and hid up in the dovecote. The Prince waited until her father came home, and told him that the lovely, mysterious girl had jumped into the dovecote. The father thought, 'Could she possibly be Ashputtel?' So he sent for the axe and the pick and broke into the dovecote. It was empty. Ashputtel had jumped down from the other side and run to the divine hazel tree. She'd removed her divine clothes and laid them on her mother's grave and the white bird had taken them away. Then she had crept back to the kitchen in her grubby grey smock. When the others came indoors, they saw only smelly little Ashputtel lying among the ashes in her crumpled clobber, with a dim little oil lamp flickering at the fireplace.

Next day, the second day of the feast, when everyone had left, Ashputtel went to the hazel tree and said:

'Shake your leaves and branches, little tree,
Shower gold and silver down on me.'

This time, the bird dropped down an even more amazing dress than before, and when Ashputtel arrived at the feast, everyone gaped wide-eyed at her beauty. The Prince had been waiting only for her. He took her by the hand immediately and danced with her and nobody else. 'She is my partner,' he said to any man who came near her. When evening came and it was time for her to leave, the Prince followed her, watching which house she would enter. But she managed to lose him and ran into the garden behind the house, where there was a fine big tree with pears growing on it. She shot up it, fast as a squirrel, and hid in its branches, and the Prince hadn't a clue where she was. When her father came, he said, 'That strange, unknown girl has escaped me again. I think she must have jumped into this pear tree.' The father thought, 'Could it possibly be Ashputtel?' So he sent for the axe again and chopped down the tree, but there was no one in it. And when they all went into the kitchen, there was Ashputtel curled up in her ashes as usual. She'd jumped down from the far side of the tree, given back her fabulous finery to the white bird, and dressed in her tatty grey smock again.

On the third day, when her parents and stepsisters had left, Ashputtel went again to her mother's grave and sang to the hazel tree:

'Shake your leaves and branches, little tree,
Shower gold and silver down on me.'

This time, the bird threw down a dress that was so sparkling and brilliant that the like of it had never been seen before, and the slippers were golden all over. When she appeared at the wedding feast in this wonderful costume, everyone was gobsmacked with admiration and wonder. The Prince danced only with her, and if anyone asked her for a dance, he said, 'She is my partner.' When evening came, Ashputtel decided to leave, and, even though the Prince wanted to come with her, she dashed away from him so speedily that he couldn't follow. But this time, the Prince had thought of a trick. He had had the whole staircase covered with tar, and as she rushed down it, her left slipper got stuck there. The Prince picked it up and looked at it closely. It was small and slim and golden all over.

The next morning, the Prince took the slipper to the house of Ashputtel's father and said to him, 'I will only marry the girl whose foot fits into the golden shoe.' Ashputtel's two stepsisters were thrilled because they had beautiful feet. The eldest took the shoe up to her bedroom to try on, with her mother watching beside her. But the shoe was too small and she couldn't fit her big toe in. And then her mother handed her a knife and said, 'Slice off your toe. Once you're Queen you won't have to bother with walking.' The girl chopped off her toe and pushed her foot into the shoe. She gritted her teeth against the terrible pain and limped back to the Prince. Seeing her foot in the golden slipper, the Prince took her as his bride and rode off with her on his horse. But their way took them past Ashputtel's mother's grave; and there were the two doves perched on the tree calling:

'Rookity-coo, Rookity-coo!
There's red blood in the golden shoe.
She chopped her toe, it was too wide,
And she is not your rightful bride.'

The Prince looked at her foot and saw the blood oozing out. He turned round his horse and rode straight back to the house and said she was the wrong girl and that the other sister must try on the shoe. So the second sister rushed up to her bedroom and managed to squeeze her toes into the shoe, but her heel wouldn't fit. Her mother passed her the knife and said, 'Carve a slice off your heel. When you're Queen you won't need to walk anywhere.' The girl hacked off a piece of her heel and forced her foot into the shoe. Then she bit her lip against the awful pain and hobbled back to the Prince. He took her as his bride, lifted her on to his horse and rode off. But as they passed the hazel tree by the grave, the two doves were perched there and called out:

> 'Rookity-coo, Rookity-coo!
> There's red blood in the golden shoe.
> She chopped her heel, it was too wide,
> And she is not your rightful bride.'

The Prince looked at the foot and saw the blood seeping from the slipper and staining her white stocking crimson. So he turned round his horse and rode the false girl home. 'She's not the right one either,' he said. 'Have you got another daughter?' 'No,' said the man. 'The only other girl is a dirty little kitchen maid whom my dead wife left behind her. She can't possibly be the bride.' The King's son asked for her to be sent for. 'No,' cried the stepmother. 'She's much too filthy. She's not fit to be looked at.' But the Prince insisted and Ashputtel had to appear. First, she scrubbed her face and hands quite clean, then went in and curtsied before the Prince. He handed her the golden shoe. Ashputtel sat down on a stool, took her slender foot out of the heavy wooden clog, and eased on the little slipper. Of course, it fitted her perfectly, and when she stood up and the Prince looked into her face he recognised her at once. She was the beautiful girl who had danced with him. 'This is my rightful bride!' he said. The stepmother and the two sisters were seething and turned ashen-faced with spite, but the Prince put Ashputtel on his horse and rode off with her. As they passed the hazel tree, the two white doves sang out:

'*Rookity-coo, Rookity-coo!*
A perfect foot in a golden shoe.
Three times has the good Prince tried,
And now he's found his rightful bride.'

When they had sung this, they flew down and perched on Ashputtel's shoulders, one on the left and one on the right, and there they stayed.

On Ashputtel's wedding day, the two nasty sisters came, hoping to suck up to her and have a share in her good fortune. As the bridal procession was entering the church, the eldest sister was on the right and the younger on the left; and the two doves flew at them and pecked out one of each of their eyes. And as they were all coming out of the church, the elder sister was on the left and the younger on the right, and the doves swooped again and stabbed out their other eyes. And so, because of their cruelty and deceit, they were punished with blindness for the rest of their long, dark, mean days.

A Riddling Tale

ow picture this: three women were turned into flowers which grew in a field.

And one of them was allowed to spend each night in her own home.

But once, when her night was nearly over, and the day was coming, forcing her back to the field to be a flower again with her companions, she said to her husband, 'If you will come early this morning and pick me, I shall be set free. I will be able to stay with you for ever.'

So her husband did this.

The riddle of the tale is: How did her husband recognise her when all three flowers were identical?

Here is the answer: Because the wife was at home

during the night, no dew fell on her, like it did on the other two.

And that is how her husband knew her. So there!

The Mouse, the Bird and the Sausage

nce upon a time, a mouse, a bird and a sausage became friends. They set up house together and lived in perfect peace, happiness and prosperity. It was the bird's job to fly to the forest every day and bring back wood. The mouse had to fetch water, light the fire, and lay the table; the sausage had to do the cooking.

But those who don't appreciate how well off they are are always tempted by something different. One day, the bird met another bird in the forest, and told him all about his excellent circumstances in life. After he'd stopped his bragging, however, the second bird called him a fool to do all the hard work, while the other two obviously had it easy at home.

When the mouse had fetched the water and made

up her fire, she went to rest in her little room until they called her to lay the table. The sausage stayed by the pot, made sure that the food was well cooked, and just before dinner time, it rolled itself once or twice through the broth to give it extra flavour. When the bird flew home and put down his load, they sat down at the table, and after a good meal, they slept well till the next morning. It really was a splendid existence for them all.

But the next day, the bird, because of what the other bird had said, refused to go into the forest. He'd been their skivvy for long enough, he said, and they weren't going to take the proverbial out of him any longer. It was time to change and arrange things in a different way. The mouse and the sausage pleaded with him; but in spite of all they said, the bird was determined to have his own way. So they drew lots to decide who would do what; and the result was that the sausage was to fetch wood, the mouse was to cook, and the bird was to draw water.

Now look what happened. The sausage went out to the forest for wood, the bird made up the fire, and the mouse put on the broth in the pot. Then the mouse and the bird waited for the sausage to come home with the wood. But the sausage was away for such a long time that they were both worried something had transpired, and the bird flew out part of the way to search for it. Not far off, he met a dog who had decided the sausage was fair game, grabbed hold of it and eaten it. The bird accused the dog of murder, but it was all to no good. The dog just said he'd found forged documents on the sausage, so it deserved to die.

The bird sadly picked up the wood and flew home to tell the mouse what had happened. They were both very distressed, but agreed to make the best of things and to stay together. And so the bird laid the table and the mouse prepared the food. She decided she would flavour it by getting into the pot like the sausage used to do; but before she had even reached the middle of the vegetables, she burned her fur and boiled her skin and lost her life in the attempt.

When the bird came to carry in their dinner, there was no sign of the cook. In his panic, the bird scattered wood everywhere, calling and searching, but the mouse couldn't be found. Because of the bird's carelessness, a fire had started and he rushed to fetch water to put it out. But the bucket fell into the well, and he tumbled in after it, and as he could not manage to scramble out again, he drowned there.

Iron Hans

here was once a King whose castle was next to a great forest which was full of all kinds of wild animals. One day, the King sent out a huntsman to shoot a deer for him, but the huntsman never returned. 'Perhaps he's had an accident,' said the King and sent out two more huntsmen to find him. But they didn't come back either. So on the third day, the King sent for all his huntsmen and ordered, 'Scour the whole forest, and don't stop searching till you find all three of them.' But none of these huntsmen came back, and not one of the pack of hounds they'd taken with them was ever seen again. From then on, no one dared to enter the forest. There it stood, dark and silent

and empty, with only a solitary eagle or hawk flying over it occasionally.

After many years, a huntsman from another country came before the King. He asked to stay at his court and volunteered to enter the dangerous forest. The King was reluctant to allow this, saying, 'The forest is unlucky. You would do no better than all the others, I fear, and you'd never get out.' But the huntsman replied, 'Sir, I will go at my own risk. I am frightened of nothing.'

So the huntsman went into the hushed, gloomy forest with his dog. The dog quickly picked up a scent and followed it, but after running a few yards, it was standing in front of a deep pool and could go no further. Suddenly, a naked arm shot out of the water, grabbed the dog and dragged it under. When the huntsman saw this, he went back and got three men to come with buckets to bail the water out of the pool. When they had scooped deep enough to see the bottom, they discovered a wild man lying there. His body was the colour of rusty iron and his hair hung over his face right down to his knees. They tied him up with ropes and pulled him away to the castle. Everyone there was astonished to see the wild man, but the King had him locked up in an iron cage in the courtyard. It was forbidden, on pain of death, to open the door, and the Queen herself was to guard the key. From then on, everyone could visit the forest in safety.

The King had a son who was eight years old. One day, the boy was playing in the courtyard with his golden ball, when it bounced into the cage. He ran up to the cage and said, 'Can I have my ball back?' 'No,' answered the wild man. 'Not unless you open this door for me.' But the boy replied, 'No, I won't do that. The King has forbidden it,' and he ran away. The next day he came back and asked for his ball, and the wild man said, 'Open my door.' But the boy refused. On the third day, the King had ridden out to hunt, and the boy came again and said, 'I can't open your door even if I wanted to, because I don't have the key.' Then the wild man replied, 'It's under your mother's pillow – you can get it from there.' The boy was so keen to have his ball back that he threw all sense and caution to the winds and fetched the key. The door was difficult to open and he hurt his finger doing it. When it was open, the wild man jumped out, tossed him his golden

ball and hurried away. The boy was frightened now, and ran behind him crying, 'Oh, wild man, don't leave, or else I shall be beaten!' The wild man turned round, picked him up, put him on his rusty shoulders and strode quickly into the forest. When the King came home, he saw the empty cage and asked the Queen what had happened. She knew nothing at all about it and searched for the key, but it had disappeared. She called for her son, but he did not reply. The King sent his servants to hunt for him in the fields and countryside, but they could not find him. Everyone could guess what had happened and the whole court was bowed down with grief.

When the wild man was back in the dark forest, he took the boy down from his shoulders and said to him, 'You will not see your mother and father again, but you can stay with me because you freed me, and I feel something for you. If you do everything I tell you to do, you shall get along fine. I have more gold and treasure than anyone else in the world.' Then he made a bed of moss for the boy to sleep on.

The next morning, the wild man took the boy to a spring and said, 'Look – this golden spring is as bright and clear as crystal. I want you to stay here and make sure nothing falls into it, or it will get polluted. Every evening I'll come back here to see if you have obeyed my instructions.' The boy sat down beside the spring. Sometimes he saw a golden fish or a golden snake in the water, and he was careful to let nothing fall in. After a while, his finger began to hurt so much that he dipped it into the water without thinking.

He quickly pulled it out again, but saw that it had turned golden all over, and he couldn't wipe it off no matter how hard he tried. In the evening, Iron Hans came back and stared at him. 'What has happened to the spring?' he asked. 'Nothing, nothing,' said the boy, hiding his finger behind his back. But the wild man said, 'You have dipped your finger into the water. I'll let it pass this time, but make sure you don't let anything touch the spring again.'

At daybreak next morning, the boy was already sitting by the spring. His finger began to hurt him again. He rubbed it on his head and, by bad luck, a hair floated down into the spring. He pulled it out quickly, but it was completely golden. Iron Hans came back and he already knew what had happened. 'You have dropped a hair into the spring,' he said. 'I'll let you watch the spring once more, but if it happens a third time then the spring is polluted and you cannot stay with me any longer.'

On the third morning, the boy sat by the spring and didn't move his finger however badly it hurt him. But the time went very slowly, and he grew bored and began staring at his own reflection in the water. And as he leaned further and further over, trying to stare right into his eyes, his long hair tumbled down from his shoulders into the spring. He pulled himself up quickly, but all the hair on his head was already golden and shone like the sun. You can imagine how terrified the poor boy was! He took out his handkerchief and tied his hair up so that the man wouldn't see it. But when he came, he already knew what had happened, and said, 'Untie your handkerchief.' Then the golden hair streamed out, and although the boy tried to make excuses for himself, it was no good. 'You have failed the test and can stay here no more. Go out alone into the world and find out what poverty is like. But because you have a good heart, and I mean you well, I will permit you one thing. If you are ever in trouble, come to the forest and shout "Iron Hans!" and I will come and help you. My powers are great – greater than you know – and I have more gold and silver than I need.'

So the Prince left the forest, and walked along the highways and byways until at last he arrived at a great city. He looked for work there, but as he had learnt no trade, he could find none. In the end, he went to the palace and asked if they would have him. The courtiers didn't know what job to give him, but they liked him and let him stay. Then the cook employed him, getting him to carry wood and water and sweep out the ashes.

One day, when no one else was to hand, the cook ordered him to carry the food in to the royal table. Because he didn't want his golden hair to be seen, the boy kept on his hat. This had never happened in the King's presence before, and he said, 'When you serve at the royal table, you must take off your hat.' 'Oh, sir,' the boy answered. 'I can't. I've got terrible dandruff.' When he heard this, the King sent for the cook and told him off, asking him what he was thinking of to employ such a boy, and ordering him to sack him at once. But the cook felt sorry for the boy and swapped him for the gardener's lad.

So now the boy had to work in the garden, even in bad weather, planting and watering and digging and hoeing. One summer's day when he was all alone, it was so warm that he took off his hat to get some fresh air on his head. The sunlight glistened and flashed on his golden hair, and the glittering rays came in through the Princess's window. She jumped up to see what it was, noticed the boy and called out to him, 'Boy! Bring me a bunch of flowers.' He quickly pulled on his hat, picked some wild flowers and tied them together. As he was carrying them up the steps, the gardener saw him and said, 'How can you take the King's daughter such common flowers? Go and find the prettiest and rarest you can for her.' 'Oh no,' replied the boy. 'Wild flowers have the strongest perfume. She'll like these best.' When he got to her room, the Princess said, 'Take off your hat. It's rude to keep it on in my presence.' 'I can't,' he said again. 'I have dandruff on my head.' But she snatched his hat and pulled it off; and then his gorgeous golden hair cascaded down to his shoulders. He tried to run out, but the Princess held him by the arm and gave him a handful of sovereigns. He went away with them, but he didn't care about the gold. So he took them to the gardener and said, 'Here, these are a present for your children to play with.' Next day, the Princess again called to him that he was to bring her a bunch of wild flowers; and when he brought them she grabbed at his hat, but he held onto it tightly with both hands. She gave him another pile of gold coins, but he didn't want to keep them and gave them to the gardener again as toys for his children. On the third day, things were just the same – she couldn't pull off his hat, and he wouldn't take her gold.

Not long after this, the whole country went to war. The King gathered his troops together, not knowing whether he'd be able to stand up to the enemy army, which was far bigger in numbers than his own. Then the gardener's boy said, 'I am grown up now and want to fight in this war too. Give me a horse.' The others laughed and said, 'Look for one when we've gone. We'll leave one behind in the stable for you.' When they had set off, he went to the stable and led

out the horse. It was lame in one foot and limped –
hobbledy-clop-clop-clop, *hobbledy-clop-clop-clop*.
But he climbed on and rode away to the dark forest.
When he came to the edge, he called out 'Iron Hans!'
three times, so loudly that his voice echoed among
all the trees. Suddenly the wild man appeared and
said, 'What is your request?' 'I need a fine, strong
horse, for I am going to war.' 'You shall have it, and
you shall have even more than you ask for.' Then the
wild man went back into the forest, and it wasn't
long before a groom appeared, leading a powerful
horse that snorted and pranced and neighed. Behind
him, there followed a great troop of warriors, all in
armour, their swords flashing in the sun. The youth
gave his lame horse to the groom, mounted the
warhorse and rode off at the head of his soldiers.
When he arrived at the battlefield, many of the King's
men had already fallen and the rest were close to
defeat. The young man galloped up with his troops of
iron, charging here and there among the enemy like
thunder and lightning, and he struck down everyone
who challenged him. They began to flee, but he
chased them and fought on till there was not one of
them left. Instead of going back to the King, though,

he took his troops the back way to the forest and called for Iron Hans. 'What is your request?' asked the wild man. 'Take back your charger and your men in armour and give me back my lame horse.' All that he asked for was done, and soon he rode – *hobbledy-clop-clop-clop* – back home.

When the King returned to the palace, his daughter came to meet him and congratulated him on winning such a victory. 'It wasn't I who won,' said her father, 'but a strange knight who came to help me with his own soldiers.' His daughter wanted to find out who the stranger was, but the King didn't know and said, 'He chased after the enemy and I never saw him again.' The Princess asked the gardener where his boy was, but he laughed and said, 'He's just limped back on his three-legged nag. The others have been teasing him and shouting out, "Here comes old hobbledy-nobbledy back again." They asked him, "Where have you been? Sleeping under a hedge all the time?" But he said, "I did better than all of you. Things would have been really bad without me." And they ridiculed him and laughed at him even harder.'

The King told his daughter, 'I will announce a great feast which will last for three days. You shall throw a golden apple, and perhaps the stranger will show himself.' When he heard about the feast, the young man returned to the forest and called Iron Hans. 'What is your request?' he asked. 'I want to catch the Princess's golden apple.' 'You practically hold it already,' said Iron Hans. 'You shall also wear a suit of red armour and ride on a magnificent chestnut horse.' When the day of the feast arrived, the young man galloped up to join the other knights, and no one recognised him. The King's daughter came forward and tossed a golden apple to the knights; but he was the only one who caught it, and as soon as he'd got it, he galloped away. On the second day, Iron Hans dressed him as a white knight on a white horse. Again he was the only one who caught the apple and, again, he galloped away with it. The King grew angry and said, 'This behaviour is disgraceful. He must come before me and tell me his name.' He gave orders that the knight was to be pursued if he rode away again, and he was to be attacked with swords if he would not return willingly.

On the third day, Iron Hans gave the young man a suit of black armour and a black horse, and again he caught the apple. But when he galloped away with it, the Kings's men chased him, and one of them rode close enough to pierce the youth's leg with the tip of his sword. He escaped from them in spite of this, but his horse reared so violently that his helmet fell from his head, and they could see his golden hair. They rode back and described all this to the King.

The next day, the Princess quizzed the gardener about his boy. 'He's working in the garden. What a weird fellow he can be. He went to the feast and only arrived back last night. Then he showed my children three golden apples he had won.' The King had the gardener's boy fetched before him, and he came with his hat jammed on his head. But the Princess went straight up to him and pulled it off, and then his golden hair fell down to his shoulders and they were all amazed by his beauty. 'Are you the knight who came to the feast every day wearing different colours and who caught the three golden apples?' asked the King. 'Yes,' he replied, 'and here are the apples.' He took them from his pocket and gave them to the King. 'If you need more proof, sir, you can see the wound your men gave me when they chased me. But I am also the knight who helped you to defeat your enemies.' 'If you can perform such marvels, then you are not a gardener's boy. Tell me now, who is your father?' 'My father is a rich and powerful King, and I have as much gold as I need.' 'I now see,' said the King, 'that I have a lot to thank you for. Is there anything I can do to reward you?' 'Yes,' he answered, 'there certainly is, sir. Give me your daughter's hand in marriage.' When she heard this, the Princess laughed and said, 'Well, he doesn't waste much time, does he! But I knew from his golden hair that he wasn't a gardener's boy!' And she went up to him and kissed him.

His mother and father came to the wedding and were overjoyed, because they had already given up hope of ever seeing him again. And as they were all sitting at the wedding feast, the music suddenly stopped, the doors burst open, and a magnificent King entered in great style. He went up to the young man, embraced him and said, 'I am Iron Hans. I was under a spell that turned me into a wild man – but you have set me free. All my treasure shall be yours.'

The Lady and the Lion

merchant was about to go on a long journey, and when he was saying goodbye to his three daughters, he asked each of them what they would like as a present. The eldest asked for pearls, the second asked for diamonds, but the youngest said, 'Father, I would like a rose.' Her father said, 'Even though it's the middle of winter, if I can find one, you shall have it.'

When it was time for him to come home again, he'd found pearls and diamonds for the two eldest, but he had searched everywhere in vain for a rose. He'd gone into many gardens asking for one, but people had just laughed and asked him if he thought roses grew in snow. This upset him, because his youngest child was his favourite. He was travelling through a forest. In the middle was a splendid castle and around the castle was a garden. Half of it was in bright summer time and the other half in gloomy winter. On one side grew the prettiest flowers, but on the other everything was dead and buried in snow. 'This is amazing!' he said to his servant, and ordered him to pick a rose from the beautiful rose bush there. But then, as they were riding away, a ferocious lion leapt out, shaking his mane and roaring so loudly that every flower in the garden shook. 'Anyone who tries to steal my roses will be eaten by me,' he roared. Then the man said, 'I'd no idea it was your garden. Please forgive me. What can I do to save my life?' The lion said, 'Nothing can save it. Only if you give me what you first meet when you go home. If you agree to do that, then I'll let you live. *And* you can take the rose for your daughter as well.' But the man hesitated and said, 'But it might be my youngest daughter. She loves me best and always runs to meet me when I get home.' His servant, though, was scared stiff and said, 'It might not be her. It could just as easily be a dog, or a cat.' So the man gave in, took the rose, and promised that the lion should have whatever he first met when he got home.

When he arrived home and went into his house, his youngest daughter ran up to him and kissed and hugged him. And she was delighted to see that he'd brought her a rose. But her father started to cry, and said, 'My darling child, this rose has cost too much. In exchange for it, I've promised to give you to a savage lion. When he has you, I'm sure he'll tear you to pieces and eat you.' He told her everything that had happened and begged her not to go. But she comforted him and said, 'Dear father, you must keep your promise. I will go there and make the lion gentle, so that I can come safely home to you.'

Next morning, she was shown the road and set off bravely for the forest. The lion, in fact, was an enchanted Prince. By day he and his people were lions, but at night they became humans again. When she arrived, she was treated kindly and taken to the castle. When night fell, the lion turned into a handsome Prince and their wedding was held with much celebration. They lived happily together but he came to her only when it was dusk and left her when morning drew near. After a while, his deep voice spoke to her from the darkness, 'Your eldest sister is getting married tomorrow and your father

is holding a feast. If you would like to go, my lions will escort you there.' She said, 'Yes, I'd love to see my father again,' and set off in the morning with the lions. There was great joy and happiness when she appeared, because everyone thought she'd been torn to shreds and killed by the wild lion. But she told them her husband was a Prince, and how happy she was. She stayed with them till the feast was over, and then returned to the forest.

When her second sister was getting married, she was invited again, and said to the Prince, 'I don't want to go alone this time. Come with me.' But he said it was too dangerous for him, and that he must never be exposed to light. He explained that if, when he was there, even a ray of candlelight fell on him, he would turn into a dove and have to fly about the world for seven long years. But she pleaded, 'Oh, do come with me. I will take special care of you and protect you from all light.' So they set off together with their little child.

She chose a room for him there, with walls so thick that no ray of light could get through. The Prince was to lock himself in there when all the candles were lit for the wedding feast. But there was a tiny crack in the door that nobody noticed. The wedding was celebrated splendidly, but when the procession came back from church with all its bright, flickering candles, it passed close by his room. A ray as fine as a single hair fell on the Prince; and as soon as it touched him he was transformed. When she came to find him, there was only a white dove in the room. The dove told her, 'Now for seven years I must fly around the globe. But for every seventh step you take, I will shed one white feather. That will show you the way, and if you follow it you can set me free.' The dove flew out of the door. She followed him. And at every seventh step, a little white feather fell down faithfully and showed her the way.

So she walked and walked through the big wild world – never even resting – and the seven years were almost over. One day, no feather fell, and when she looked up, the dove had disappeared. She thought to herself, 'No one human can help me with this.' So she climbed up to the sun and said to him, 'You shine into every crack, over every mountain – have you seen a white dove flying?' 'No,' replied the sun. 'I have not. But I'll give you this casket. Open it when you are most in need.' She thanked the sun and walked on until it was evening. The moon rose and she asked her, 'You shine all night, over all the fields and the forests – have you seen a white dove flying?' 'No,' said the moon. 'I have not. But I'll give you this egg. Break it when you are in great need.' She thanked the moon and walked on until the night wind began to blow on her. She said to it, 'You blow on every tree and under every leaf – have you seen a white dove flying?' 'No,' said the night wind. 'I have not. But I'll ask the other three winds if they've seen it.' The east and the west winds came and had seen nothing, but the south wind breathed, 'I saw the white dove. It has flown to the Red Sea and has become a lion again, because the seven years are now up. The lion is fighting with a dragon, but the dragon is really an enchanted Princess.' Then the night wind said to her, 'Follow my advice. Go to the Red Sea. On the right bank you'll see some tall reeds. Count them, break off number eleven, and hit the dragon with it. Then the lion will be able to overpower it and both of them will become human again. When this happens, set off at once with your beloved Prince and travel home over land and sea.'

So the poor girl wandered on, and found everything just as the night wind had said. She counted the reeds by the sea, snapped off the eleventh, and struck the dragon with it. Then the lion overpowered it and they both became human immediately. But when the Princess, who had been the dragon, was freed from the spell, she seized the Prince by the arm and carried him off. The pilgrim, who had followed and walked so far, sat down and wept. But in the end, she found her courage and said, 'I will still travel as far as the wind blows and as long as the cock crows until I find my love again.' And she set off along long, hard roads until at last she arrived at the castle where the two of them were living together. She discovered soon there was going to be a feast to celebrate their wedding, but she said, 'Heaven will help me.' Then she opened the casket that the sun had given her. Inside was a dress as dazzling as the sun itself. So she put it on, and went up to the castle. Everyone stared at her in astonishment, even the bride. In fact, the bride liked the dress so much that she wanted it for a wedding dress and asked if it was for sale. 'Not for money or land,' the girl answered, 'but for flesh and blood.' When the bride asked what she meant, the girl said, 'Let me sleep a night in the same room as the bridegroom.' The bride wouldn't agree, but she wanted the dress so badly that at last she said yes. But she told her page to give the Prince a sleeping draught.

When it was night, and the Prince was already sleeping, the girl was led into his bedchamber. She sat on the bed and said, 'I have followed after you for seven long years. I have asked the sun and the moon and the four winds for news of you. I have helped

241

you against the dragon. Do you really forget me?'
But the Prince was fast asleep and only thought he
heard the wind murmuring and rustling in the trees.
When morning came, she was taken out of his room
and had to hand over the golden dress. And because
it had all been no use, she wandered sadly into the
fields, sat down, and cried. While she was sitting
there, she remembered the egg which the moon had
given to her. So she cracked it open and out came
a clucking hen with twelve little chickens made of
gold. They ran about chirping and cheeping, then
crept under their mother's wings. They were the most
adorable sight anyone could see. She stood up and
drove them through the field until the bride looked
out of her window. The tiny chickens delighted her so
much that she hurried down and asked if they were
for sale. 'Not for money or land, but for flesh and
blood. Let me sleep another night in the bridegroom's
chamber.' The bride said yes, but she intended to
drug him like before. But when the Prince was going
to bed, he asked the page what the murmuring and
rustling in the night had been. Then the page told
him everything: that he'd been forced to give him
a sleeping potion, because a strange girl had slept

secretly in his room; and that he was supposed to give him another one tonight. The Prince said, 'Pour the sleeping draught away.' At night, the girl was led in again, and when she started to tell him all the sad things that had happened and how faithful to him she had been, he immediately recognised the voice of his beloved wife. He jumped up and cried, 'Now I am really released! I have been in a dream, because the strange Princess has bewitched me to make me forget you. But heaven has sent you to me in time, my dear love.' Then they both crept away from the castle, secretly in the dark, because they were afraid of the strange Princess. Together they journeyed all the way home. There they found their child, who had grown tall and beautiful, and they all lived happily until the end of their days and nights.

The Magic Table,
the Gold-Donkey and the
Cudgel in the Sack

n a time before you were born,
there was a tailor who had
three sons and one goat. The
goat provided milk for the four
of them, so every day it had to
be taken out to graze, and fed
well. The sons took turns in doing this. One day,
the eldest son took the goat to the churchyard. There
was lots of succulent greenery there and he let her
feed and jump around. At dusk, when it was time to
go home, he asked her, 'Goat, have you had enough
to eat?' And the goat replied:

'I've had enough,
I'm full of the stuff. Beh! Beh!'

'Let's go home then,' said the boy, and he took hold of her halter, led her back to her shed and tied her up safely. 'Well,' said his father, 'did you feed the goat properly?' 'Oh yes,' said his son, 'she's had enough – she's full of the stuff.' But his father wanted to check for himself, so he went down to the shed, patted the precious goat, and inquired, 'Goat, are you sure you've had enough to eat?' The goat replied:

> *'There was no grass to eat*
> *Where he took me to feed.*
> *Hard stones on the ground*
> *Were all that I found. Beh! Beh!'*

'What's this I hear!' thundered the tailor. He ran back up and said to his eldest son, 'You liar! Why did you tell me you'd given the goat enough to eat when you've let her starve?' In his fury, he grabbed his yardstick from the wall and thrashed his son out of the house.

Next day, it was the second son's turn. He picked a good place by the garden hedge with lots of fresh, moist greenery, and the goat munched it right down to the ground. At home time, the boy asked,

'Goat, have you had enought to eat?' and the goat answered:

> *'I've had enough,*
> *I'm full of the stuff. Beh! Beh!'*

'Let's get home then,' said the boy, and he led her back and tied her securely in the shed. 'Well,' said his father, 'did you feed the goat well?' 'Certainly,' said his son. 'She's had enough – she's full of the stuff.' But the tailor went down to the shed to make sure, and said, 'Goat, have you had enough to eat?' The goat answered:

> *'There was no grass to eat*
> *Where he took me to feed.*
> *Hard stones on the ground*
> *Were all that I found. Beh! Beh!'*

'The heartless big lump!' yelled the tailor. 'Letting such a fine animal starve!' And he ran up and seized his stick and beat his poor son out of the house.

Now it was the youngest son's turn, and he was determined to do things properly. He chose a spot with abundant leafy bushes and let the goat nibble away to her heart's content. In the evening, he asked, 'Goat, are you quite, quite sure you've had enough?' The goat replied:

'I've had enough,
I'm full of the stuff. Beh! Beh!'

'Let's go home then,' said the boy, and he led her to her shed and tied her up. 'Well,' asked his father, 'have you fed the goat properly?' 'Absolutely,' said his son, 'she's had enough – she's full of the stuff.' But the tailor didn't trust him, and went down to ask, 'Goat, are you sure you've had enough to eat?' And the wicked goat said:

'There was no grass to eat
Where he took me to feed.
Hard stones on the ground
Were all that I found. Beh! Beh!'

'You pack of liars!' roared the tailor. 'All three of you are deceitful and undutiful. Well, you'll not make a fool out of me any more!' And quite crimson in the face with rage, he rushed up and thwacked the poor boy's back with the stick so hard that he ran out of the house.

Now the old tailor was all alone with his goat. Next morning, he went down to the shed, stroked the goat and said, 'Come along, my little pet, I'll take you out to graze myself.' He led her away to a place where there were green hedges and long grasses and all the things goats love to eat. 'Now you can eat your fill for once,' he said, and let her chomp away till evening. Then he asked, 'Dear goat, have you had enough to eat?' And the goat replied:

> *'I've had enough,*
> *I'm full of the stuff. Beh! Beh!'*

'Come along home then,' said the tailor; and he led her to her shed and tied her up. As he was leaving, he turned round and said, 'Now for once I *know* you've really had plenty to eat.' But he had no more luck with the goat than his sons had had, and the bad goat bleated out:

> *'There was no grass to eat*
> *Where you took me to feed.*

Hard stones on the ground
Were all that I found. Beh! Beh!'

When the tailor heard this, he was horrified and realised how unjustly he'd treated his three sons. 'You ungrateful beast!' he screamed at the goat. 'Just you wait! I'll make a mark on you that'll stop you showing your treacherous face among respectable people!' He rushed upstairs, grabbed his razor, lathered the goat's head, and shaved it as smooth as a billiard ball. And because the stick would have been too good for it, he fetched his whip and flogged her so badly that she went leaping away for her life.

So the tailor was now all alone in his empty house. He became terribly sad and longed to have his sons back again, but nobody knew where they were. The eldest boy had become a joiner's apprentice. He was hard-working and conscientious, and when his apprenticeship was over and it was time for him to move on, his master gave him a little table. It was made of wood and looked perfectly ordinary, but there was something special about it. If you put it before you and said 'Table, be laid!' this splendid little table would immediately cover itself with a clean tablecloth; and there would be a plate with a knife and fork, as many dishes of good hot food as there was room for, and a big, robust, glowing glass of ruby wine to warm the chilliest heart. The young man thought to himself, 'Now you're sorted for your whole life,' and he journeyed happily round the world. He didn't have to bother whether any inn he came to was good or bad or whether or not he could find a decent meal. Sometimes, if he was in

the mood, he didn't even stay at an inn, but camped out in the fields and woods. He'd take the table from his back, set it before him and say 'Table, be laid!' and it gave him all the food and drink he wanted. Eventually, the boy decided to return home to his father. He thought, 'He won't be angry with me after all this time, and now that I have a magic table, he's sure to welcome me!' So he set off home, and one evening he came to an inn that was full of guests. They made him welcome and asked him to join them at their meal, otherwise there'd be no food left for him. 'No,' said the young joiner, 'I won't take your last few mouthfuls. You shall be my guests instead.' They thought he was joking with them and they laughed. But he set down his table in the middle of the room and said, 'Table, be laid!' At once, it was covered with much better food than the landlord of the inn could even dream of, and the delicious smell of it made their noses twitch. 'Help yourselves, my friends,' said the joiner, and they all moved up their chairs, grasped their knives and forks, and tucked in happily. The amazing thing was that as soon as one dish was empty, another full one took its place immediately.

The landlord stood watching silently from a corner. 'I could do with a cook like that here at my inn,' he thought. The joiner and his guests ate and drank and laughed and talked late into the night. But finally they went to bed, and the young man lay down to sleep as well, putting his magic table against the wall. The landlord's envy kept him awake. He remembered that he had a table which looked exactly the same up in his attic. So very quietly he fetched it, crept in, and swapped it for the magic table.

Next morning, the joiner paid his bill, lifted the table onto his back – never dreaming that it was the wrong one – and set off for his father's house. He arrived home at midday and his father was overjoyed to see him. 'Well, well, well, my dear boy,' he said. 'What have you learnt?' 'Father, I've become a joiner.' 'That's a worthwhile trade,' replied his father, 'and what have you brought back from your travels?' 'Father, I've brought the most wonderful thing – a little table.' The old man examined the table all over and said, 'Well, you've made no work of art here. It's just a shabby old table.' 'But it's a magic table,' said the son. 'When I put it down in front of me and tell it to lay itself, the finest food and wine appear and gladden the heart. Just ask all our friends and relatives over and we'll give them a real treat. They can eat and drink as much as they want.'

So when all the guests had assembled, he put his little table in the middle of the room and said, 'Table, be laid!' But this table did nothing. It stayed just as bare and wooden and still as any other table that doesn't understand when it's spoken to. Then the poor joiner realised what had happened at the inn; and he stood there ashamed and embarrassed that everyone would think he was a liar. His relations had a good old laugh at him, but had to go home with empty bellies. His father got out some cloth and went on tailoring, and the son went to work for a master joiner.

The second son had fetched up at a mill and apprenticed himself to the miller. When he'd finished his time, his master said, 'Because you've been such a good worker, I'm going to give you a donkey. He's very special. He doesn't pull a cart and he won't carry sacks of flour either.' 'Then what's the use of him?' asked the young man. 'He spits out gold,' said the miller. 'If you stand him on a cloth and say "Jobaloo", this magnificent creature will produce gold coins for you from both ends!' 'This is wonderful,' said the young man. And he thanked his master and set off into the world. If ever he needed gold, he only had to say 'Jobaloo' to his donkey. Out would pour a shower of gold coins and he just had to bend down and pick them up. Because his purse was always full of gold, he bought the best of everything. After travelling for a time, he decided to visit his father. He thought, 'When I turn up with the gold-donkey, he'll forget his anger and make me welcome.' On his way home, he stopped at the same inn as his brother. He was leading his donkey, and the landlord was about to take it for him, when he said, 'Don't bother yourself, landlord. I'll take my donkey to the stable myself. I like to know where he is.' The landlord thought this was strange, and that a man who had to tie up his own donkey wasn't likely to have much money to spend. But when the young man pulled two gold pieces from his pocket and told him to buy him something good for supper, the landlord opened his eyes wide and hurried away to buy the best food and drink. After dinner, his guest asked him if he owed him anything, and the greedy landlord thought he might as well charge double and asked for two more gold pieces. The boy put his hand in his pocket, but it was empty, so he said, 'Hang on, landlord, I'll just go and get some more gold.' But he took the tablecloth with him.

The landlord couldn't understand this at all, so he secretly followed the boy. He crept along and discovered that his guest had bolted the stable door. Filled with curiosity he peered in through a gap in the wood. The young man spread the tablecloth under the donkey, called out 'Jobaloo', and suddenly the beast began to throw out gold from both ends – showers and showers of it. 'Well, who would believe it,' said the landlord, rubbing his eyes in amazement. 'That's a quick way to make gold. I could use a moneybag like that.' The guest paid for his dinner and went to bed; but the landlord sneaked down to the stables overnight, led the gold-donkey away and tied up another donkey in its place.

Early next morning, the boy set off, thinking he still had his own gold-donkey. He arrived home at midday and his father gave him a warm welcome. 'Well, well, well, my boy, and what have you become?' 'I am a miller, Father.' 'And what have you brought back with you from your travels?' 'Just a donkey.' 'We're all right for donkeys around here,' said the father. 'It would have been better if you'd brought a decent goat.' 'But this is no ordinary donkey, Father, it's a gold-donkey. When I say "Jobaloo", this wonderful creature drops down a whole tablecloth of gold coins. Ask all our friends and relatives round and I'll make every one of them rich.' 'That'll do me,' said the tailor. 'I won't need to work my old fingers to the bone with this needle any more.' And he ran round himself and invited all their relations.

As soon as everyone was there, the son asked them to make a space, spread out a cloth and led in the donkey. 'Watch this, everybody!' he said proudly, and called out 'Jobaloo!' But what landed on the white cloth was certainly not gold, and it was obvious that this donkey could pump out no more than any other old donkey. The poor young miller was mortified. He knew that he'd been tricked and just had to apologise to his relatives, who trudged home as poor as they'd always been. So the old man had to take up his needle again and the boy had to get a job with a miller.

The youngest son had apprenticed himself to a turner, and because this is such a skilled trade, he took longest to learn it. His brothers wrote him a letter, telling him of their bad luck and how the villainous landlord had stolen their magic gifts on the night before they got home. When the young turner had completed his time and was setting out to travel, his master rewarded him for his fine, honest work with a sack. 'It's got a cudgel inside,' he said. 'Well, I can sling the sack over my shoulder and make good use of it,' said the boy, 'but the cudgel will just make it heavy to carry. What use is it?' 'Plenty of use,' said his master. 'If anyone ever does you any harm at all, just say "Cudgel, out of the sack!" and the cudgel will jump out at whoever's there and dance so madly on their backs that they won't be able to walk for a week. And it won't stop till you say "Cudgel, back in the sack!"' The young miller said thank you, chucked the sack over his shoulder, and after that, if anyone gave him any trouble, he'd say 'Cudgel, out of the sack!' At once the cudgel would leap out and give their coats or jackets such a fierce dusting – while they were still wearing them – and it beat their backs so fast that before the next man knew what was to do it was his turn already.

Eventually, the boy arrived at the bad landlord's inn. He put his sack down in front of him on the table, and started to talk about all the miraculous things he'd seen on his travels. 'Oh yes,' he yawned, 'you come across magic tables and gold-donkeys and all that sort of thing – excellent in their way and I've nothing against them – but they're peanuts compared to the treasure I've got in my sack here.' The landlord listened excitedly and wondered what it could be. He thought, 'Perhaps his sack is filled with jewels. If it is, *I* should have them as well. Twice is nice, but thrice is nicer.'

At bedtime, his guest lay down on the bench and put his sack under his head for a pillow. When the landlord thought he was sound asleep, he sneaked up and began tugging very gently and slowly at the sack. His sly plan was to pull it out and put another one in its place. Of course, this was exactly what the turner wanted, and just as the landlord was about to give one last tug, he called out, 'Cudgel, out of the sack!' Quick as anger, the cudgel was out and giving the landlord a terrible tattooing. The landlord screamed and howled, but the more noise he made, the more the cudgel tap danced on his back, till finally he fell to the ground and stayed there. Then the young man said, 'Unless you give back the magic table and the gold-donkey, the painful polka will begin again.' 'Oh no,' moaned the landlord – very humbly now – 'I'll give you the lot, sir, honestly – just tell that hideous thing to get back in its sack.' 'Very well, I shall give you mercy as well as justice,' said the young man, 'but just you mind your step in future.' Then he called out, 'Cudgel, back in the sack!' and the cudgel had a rest.

Next morning, the turner went home to his father with the magic table and the gold-donkey. His father was delighted to see him, and asked him what he had learnt. 'I am a turner, dear Father,' he said. 'A very skilful trade,' said the old tailor. 'And what have you brought home from your travels?' 'Something very valuable, Father. A cudgel in a sack.' 'A cudgel?' scoffed his father. 'What for? You can hack one off the nearest tree.' The son smiled. 'Not one like this, dear Father. When I say, "Cudgel, out of the sack!" the cudgel jumps out and bangs away at anyone who's giving me trouble. And it doesn't stop its bruising dance until they beg for mercy. Look, Father, with this cudgel I've got back the magic table and the gold-donkey that were stolen from my brothers. So send for both of them and invite all our friends and relations. I'll fill their bellies with food and drink and their pockets with gold.' The old tailor still wasn't sure about this, but he did as his youngest son asked.

When they were all together, the turner put a cloth

down on the floor, led in the gold-donkey, and said to his brother, 'Now, my dear brother, speak to your donkey!' The miller called out 'Jobaloo!' and there and then it began to rain gold coins on the cloth. The donkey didn't stop till everyone's pockets were bulging. (I bet you'd have liked to have been there too!) Then the turner fetched the little table and said, 'Speak to your table, my good brother.' As soon as the joiner cried 'Table be laid!' the table was crowded with every delicious dish and the best wine. Then they had a feast the like of which had never been known in the poor tailor's house, and the whole family stayed together till late at night, having the most wonderful party. The tailor locked away his needle and thread and yardstick, and lived long and happy and prosperous with his three fine sons.

But what about the wicked goat whose fault it was that the three sons had been thrown out of their home? Listen to this. She was so ashamed of being bald that she ran to a fox-hole and crawled in to hide there. When the fox came home, he saw two huge yellowy eyes gleaming at him in the darkness. He was so scared that he ran away. The bear met him and he looked so terrified that he asked, 'What's the matter, brother fox?' 'Oh,' said the fox. 'There's a terrible monster squatting in my earth-hole, glowering at me with glowing eyes.' 'We'll soon get rid of it,' said the bear, and he went with the fox to his hole and peeped in. But when he saw the fiery eyes, he was scared as well, and ran away. The bee met him, and saw that he looked upset and said, 'Bear, that's a very worried face you have. What's the matter?' 'Oh, it's awful,' said the bear. 'There's a savage beast with burning eyes sitting in brother fox's house and we can't get it out.' The bee said, 'Poor old bear. I know I'm only a little thing that you hardly ever notice, but I think I can help you.' The bee flew into the fox's hole, landed on the goat's bald head and stung her so badly that she leapt up bleating, *'Beh! Beh! Beh!'* and ran out into the big wide world like a mad creature. And no one knows where she fetched up to this very day.

Little Red-Cap

here was once a delicious little girl who was loved by everyone who saw her, but most of all by her grandmother, who was always wondering what treat to give the sweet child next. Once she sent her a little red cap which suited her so well that she wouldn't wear anything else and she was known from then on as Little Red-Cap.

One day her mother said, 'Little Red-Cap, here are some cakes and a bottle of best wine. Take them to Grandmother. She's been poorly and is still a bit weak and these will do her good. Now, hurry up before it gets too hot. And mind how you go, like a good little girl. And don't go wandering off the path or you'll fall over and break the wine bottle – because there will be none left for Grandmother if you do. And when you go into her room, make sure you say "Good morning" nicely, instead of peeping into every corner first!'

Little Red-Cap held her mother's hand and said, 'Don't worry, I'll do everything just as you say.'

Her grandmother lived out in the wood, a half an hour's walk from the village, and as soon as Little Red-Cap stepped into the wood, a wolf saw her. Because she didn't know what a wicked animal it was, she wasn't afraid of it.

'Good morning, Little Red-Cap,' it said.

'Thank you, Wolf.'

'And where might you be going so early?'

'To my grandmother's house.'

'And what's that you're carrying in your apron?'

'Cakes and wine. We were baking yesterday – and my poor grandmother has been ill, so these will strengthen her.'

'Where does Grandmother live, Little Red-Cap?'

'She lives a quarter of an hour's walk from here, under the three big oak trees. Her house has hazel hedges near it. I'm sure you know it.'

But the wolf was thinking to itself, 'How young and sweet and tender she is. I could eat her. She'll make a plumper mouthful for my jaws than the old woman.

If I am cunning, though, I can scoff the pair of them!'
So it walked beside Little Red-Cap for a bit, and then
said, 'Look, Little Red-Cap. Open your eyes and see!
There are beautiful flowers all around us. And there's
wonderful birdsong that you don't even listen to. You
just plod straight ahead as though you were going to
school – and yet the woods are such fun!'

So Little Red-Cap gazed around her and when she
saw the sunbeams seeming to wink at her among
the trees, and when she saw the tempting flowers
leading away from the straight path, she thought,
'Grandmother will be very pleased if I pick her a
bunch of lovely fresh flowers. And it's still early, so I've
got plenty of time.' So she ran from the path, among
the trees, gathering her flowers, and she kept seeing
prettier and prettier flowers, which led her deeper and
deeper into the wood.

But the wily wolf ran fast and straight to the
grandmother's house and knocked on the door.

'Who's there?' called out Grandmother.

'Only Little Red-Cap, bringing you cake and wine.
Open the door.'

'Lift the latch. I'm too feeble to get up.'

So the wolf lifted the latch and the door flew open

and without even a word it leapt onto the old woman's bed and gobbled her up. Then it pulled her clothes and her nightcap over its wolfy fur, crawled into her bed and closed the curtains.

All this time, Little Red-Cap had been trotting about among the flowers and when she'd picked as many as her arms could hold, she remembered her grandmother and hurried off to her house. She was surprised to see that the door was open and as soon as she stepped inside she felt very strange and said to herself, 'Oh dear, I always look forward to seeing Grandmother, so why do I feel so nervous today?'

'Good morning?' she said, but there was no reply. So she walked over to the bed and drew back the curtains.

Grandmother lay there with her nightcap pulled right down over her face, looking very peculiar indeed.

'Oh, Grandmother, what big ears you have!'

'The better to hear you with, my sweet.'

'Oh, Grandmother, what big eyes you have!'

'The better to see you with, my love.'

'Oh, Grandmother, what big hands you have!'

'The better to touch you with, my precious.'

'But Grandmother, what a terrible big mouth you have.'

'The better to eat you.'

And as soon as the words had left its drooling lips, the wolf made one leap from the bed and gobbled up poor Little Red-Cap. When it had had its fill, the wolf dragged itself onto the bed, fell fast asleep and started to snore very loudly. The Huntsman was just passing the house and thought, 'How loudly the old woman is snoring. I'd better see if something is wrong.' So he went into the house and when he reached the bed he saw the wolf spread out in it.

'So you've come here, you old sinner. I've wanted to catch you for a long, long time.' The Huntsman took aim with his gun and was about to shoot when it flashed through his mind that the wolf might have swallowed the grandmother whole and that she might still be saved. So instead of firing, he got a good pair of scissors and began to snip the belly of the sleeping wolf.

After two snips he saw the bright red colour of the little red cap. Two snips, three snips, four snips more and out jumped Little Red-Cap, crying, 'Oh, how frightened I've been! It's so dark inside the wolf!' And then out came the grandmother, hardly breathing, but still alive. Little Red-Cap rushed outside and quickly fetched some big stones and they filled the wolf's belly with them. When the wolf woke up, it tried to run away, but the great stones in its evil gut were too heavy and it dropped down dead.

When this happened, all three were delighted. The Huntsman skinned the wolf and went home with its pelt. The grandmother ate the cake and drank the wine and soon began to feel much better. And Little Red-Cap promised herself, 'Never so long as I live will I wander off the path into the woods when my mother has warned me not to.'

Two Households

here are you going?'

'To Walpe.'

'You to Walpe, me to Walpe, knyd, knyd, together we'll go.'

'Got a man? What's his name?'

'Dan.'

'Your man Dan, my man Dan, you to Walpe, me to Walpe, knyd, knyd, together we'll go.'

'Got a child? How's he styled?'

'Wild.'

'Your child Wild, my child Wild, your man Dan, my man Dan, you to Walpe, me to Walpe, knyd, knyd, together we'll go.'

'Got a cradle? What's its label?'

'Hippodadle.'

'Your cradle Hippodadle, my cradle Hippodadle,

your child Wild, my child Wild, your man Dan, my man Dan, you to Walpe, me to Walpe, knyd, knyd, together we'll go.'

'Got a servant? What's his title?'

'Stay-a-Bed Bone-Idle.'

'Your servant Stay-a-Bed Bone-Idle, my servant, Stay-a-Bed Bone-Idle, your cradle Hippodadle, my cradle Hippodadle, your child Wild, my child Wild, your man Dan, my man Dan, you to Walpe, me to Walpe, knyd, knyd, together we'll go.'

The Fox and the Geese

ne day the fox came to a meadow and there sat a flock of fine geese. The fox smiled and said, 'My timing is perfect. There you are all sitting together quite beautifully, so that I can eat you up one after the other.' The geese cackled with terror, jumped up and began to wail and plead piteously for their lives. But the fox would have none of it and said, 'Begging is useless. There is no mercy to be had. You must die.'

At last, one of the geese stepped up and said, 'If we poor geese are to lose our healthy young lives, then please allow us one last prayer so that we do not die with our sins on our conscience. One final prayer and then we will line up in a row so that you can always pick the plumpest first.'

The fox thought, 'Yes, that's a reasonable request, and a pious one too.'

'Pray away, geese. I'll wait till you are finished.'

So the first goose began a good long prayer, for ever saying 'Ga! Ga!' and, as she wouldn't stop, the second didn't wait her turn but started praying away also. 'Ga! Ga!' The third and the fourth followed her – 'Ga! Ga!' – and soon they were all praying and honking and cackling together.

When they have finished their prayers, this story shall be continued further, but at the moment they are still very busy praying. 'Ga! Ga! Ga! Ga! Ga! Ga!'

Clever Hans

ans's mother said, 'Where are you off to Hans?' Hans said, 'To see Gretel.' 'Behave well, Hans.' 'Oh, I'll behave well. Goodbye, Mother.' 'Goodbye, Hans.'

Hans goes to Gretel. 'Good day, Gretel.' 'Good day, Hans. What have you brought that's good?' 'I've brought nowt. I want to have something given me.' Gretel presents Hans with a needle. 'Goodbye, Gretel.' 'Goodbye, Hans.'

Hans takes the needle, sticks it into a hay cart, follows the cart home. 'Good evening, Mother.' 'Good evening, Hans. Where have you been?' 'With Gretel.' 'What did Gretel give you?' 'Gave me a needle.' 'Where is the needle, Hans?' 'Stuck in the hay cart.' 'That was poorly done, Hans. You should have stuck the needle in your sleeve.' 'Not to worry. Do better next time.'

'Where are you off to, Hans?' 'To Gretel's, Mother.' 'Behave well, Hans.' 'Oh, I'll behave well. Goodbye, Mother.' 'Goodbye, Hans.'

Hans goes to Gretel. 'Good day, Gretel.' 'Good day, Hans. What have you brought that's good?' 'I've brought nowt. I want to have something given to me.' Gretel presents Hans with a knife. 'Goodbye, Gretel.' 'Goodbye, Hans.'

Hans takes the knife, sticks it in his sleeve, and goes home. 'Good evening, Mother.' 'Good evening, Hans. Where have you been?' 'With Gretel.' 'What did you take her?' 'Took nowt. Got given something.' 'What did Gretel give you?' 'Gave me a knife.' 'Where is the knife, Hans?' 'Stuck in my sleeve.' 'That was poorly done, Hans. You should have put the knife in your pocket.' 'Not to worry. Do better next time.'

'Where are you off to, Hans?' 'To Gretel, Mother.' 'Behave well, Hans.' 'Oh, I'll behave well. Goodbye, Mother.' 'Goodbye, Hans.'

Hans goes to Gretel. 'Good day, Gretel.' 'Good day, Hans. What good thing have you brought?'

'I've brought nowt. I want something given me.' Gretel presents Hans with a young goat.

Hans takes the goat, ties its legs and puts it in his pocket. When he gets home it has suffocated. 'Good evening, Mother.' 'Good evening, Hans. Where have you been?' 'With Gretel.' 'What did you take her?' 'Took nowt. Got given something.' 'What did Gretel give you?' 'She gave me a goat.' 'Where is the goat, Hans?' 'Put it in my pocket.' 'That was poorly done, Hans. You should have put a rope round the goat's neck.' 'Not to worry. Do better next time.'

'Where are you off to, Hans?' 'To Gretel, Mother.' 'Behave well, Hans.' 'Oh, I'll behave well. Goodbye, Mother.' 'Goodbye, Hans.'

Hans goes to Gretel. 'Good day, Gretel.' 'Good day, Hans. What good thing have you brought?' 'I've brought nowt. I want something given me.' Gretel presents Hans with a piece of bacon. 'Goodbye, Gretel.' 'Goodbye, Hans.'

Hans takes the bacon, ties it to a rope and drags it away behind him. The dogs come sniffing and scoff the bacon. When he gets home he has the rope in his hand with nothing at the end of it. 'Good evening, Mother.' 'Good evening, Hans. Where have you been?'

'With Gretel.' 'What did you take her?' 'Took nowt. Got given something.' 'What did Gretel give you?' 'Gave me a bit of bacon.' 'Where is the bacon, Hans?' 'I tied it to a rope, pulled it home. Dogs had it.' 'That was poorly done, Hans. You should have carried the bacon on your head.' 'Not to worry. Do better next time.'

'Where are you off to, Hans?' 'To Gretel, Mother.' 'Behave well, Hans.' 'Oh, I'll behave well. Goodbye, Mother.' 'Goodbye, Hans.'

Hans goes to Gretel. 'Good day, Gretel.' 'Good day, Hans. What have you brought me that's good?' 'I've brought nowt. I want something given me.' Gretel presents Hans with a calf. 'Goodbye, Gretel.' 'Goodbye, Hans.'

Hans takes the calf and puts it on his head. The calf gives his face a kicking. 'Good evening, Mother.' 'Good evening, Hans. Where have you been?' 'With Gretel.' 'What did you take her?' 'Took nowt. Got given something.' 'What did Gretel give you?' 'A calf.' 'Where is the calf, Hans?' 'I put it on my head and it kicked my face.' 'That was poorly done, Hans. You should have led the calf and put it in the stable.' 'Not to worry. Do better next time.'

'Where are you off to, Hans?' 'To Gretel, Mother.'

'Behave well, Hans.' 'Oh, I'll behave well. Goodbye, Mother.' 'Goodbye, Hans.'

Hans goes to Gretel. 'Good day, Gretel.' 'Good day, Hans. What good thing have you brought?' 'I've brought nowt. I want something given me.' Gretel says to Hans, 'I will come with you.'

Hans takes Gretel, ties her to a rope, leads her to the stable and binds her tight. Then Hans goes to his mother. 'Good evening, Mother.' 'Good evening, Hans. Where have you been?' 'With Gretel.' 'What did you take her?' 'I took her nowt.' 'What did Gretel give you?' 'She gave me nowt. She came back with me.' 'Where have you left Gretel?' 'I led her by the rope, tied her up in the stable, and scattered a bit of grass for her.' 'That was poorly done, Hans. You should have cast warm eyes on her.' 'Not to worry. Will do better.'

Hans marched into the stable, cut out all the calves' and sheep's eyes, and threw them in Gretel's face. Then Gretel became very angry, tore herself loose and ran away. Gretel was finished with Hans.

Knoist and His Three Sons

omewhere between Werrel and Soist lived a bloke whose name was Knoist and he had three sons. One was blind, the other was lame and the third was stark bollock-naked. Once upon a time, they went into a field and there they saw a hare. The blind one shot it, the lame one caught it and the naked one put it in his pocket. Then they came to a mighty great lake, upon which three boats bobbed.

One sailed, the other sank, and the third had no bottom. All three lads got into the one with no bottom. Then they came to a mighty great forest in the middle of which was a mighty great tree in the middle of which was a mighty great church. Inside the church was a sexton made of beech wood and a parson made of box wood, and the pair of them sprinkled out holy water with cudgels.

> '*He'll be happy if he's the one*
> '*Who can from Holy Water run.*'

Sweet Porridge

nce upon a different time there was a very good little girl who lived with her mother; but they were so poor they had nothing left to eat. So the little girl went into the forest. An old woman met her, who knew of her troubles. She gave her a small pot which when she said, 'Cook, little pot, cook!' would cook sweet and nourishing porridge. When she said 'Stop, little pot!' it would stop cooking.

The girl took the pot home to her mother and from then on they were no longer hungry and ate good sweet porridge whenever they wanted.

One day, when the little girl had gone out, her mother said, 'Cook, little pot, cook!' And it cooked away and she ate till she was quite full up. She wanted the pot to stop cooking then, but she didn't know the words. So it carried on cooking, cooking, until the porridge spilled over the brim; and it carried on cooking, cooking, until the kitchen was full, then the whole house, then the house next door, then the whole street; and it carried on cooking, cooking, as though it wanted to satisfy the hunger of the whole world. It caused the greatest inconvenience and distress, but no one knew how to stop it.

At last, when there was only one single house left, like one spud on a plate, the little girl came home and said, 'Stop, little pot!' And it stopped and gave up cooking. But anyone who wanted to return to the town had to eat their way back in.

The Hare and the Hedgehog

his tale, my splendid young listeners, may seem to you to be false, but it really is true, because I heard it from my grandfather, and when he told it he always said, 'It must be true, my dear, or else no one could tell it to you.' This is the story.

One Sunday morning around harvest time, just as the buckwheat was blooming, the sun was shining, the breeze was blowing, the larks were singing, the bees were buzzing, the folk were off to church in their Sunday best, everything that lived was happy and the hedgehog was happy too.

The hedgehog was stood by his own front door, arms akimbo, relishing the morning and singing a song to himself half-aloud. It was no better or worse

282

a song than the songs which hedgehogs usually sing on a Sabbath morning. His wife was inside, washing and drying the children, and he suddenly decided that he'd take a stroll in the field and see how his turnips were doing. The turnips grew beside the hedgehog's house and the hedgehog family were accustomed to eating them – because of this he thought of them as his own. The hedgehog clicked shut his front door and set off for the field. He hadn't gone very far, and was just turning round the sloe bush, which grows outside the field, to go up into the turnip field, when he noticed the hare. The hare was out and about on a similar errand to visit his cabbages. The hedgehog called out a friendly good morning. But the hare, a distinguished gentleman in his own way, was hoity-toity and gave the hedgehog a snooty look. He didn't say good morning back, but spoke in a very contemptuous manner:

'What brings you scampering about in the field so early in the morning?'

'I'm taking a walk,' said the hedgehog.

'A walk!' said the hare with a haughty sneer. 'Surely you can think of a better use for those legs of yours.'

These words made the hedgehog livid with rage,

for he couldn't bear any reference to his legs, which are naturally crooked.

The hedgehog said, 'You seem to think you can do more with your legs than I can with mine.'

'That's exactly what I think.'

'That can soon be put to the test. I'll bet that if we run a race, I shall beat you.'

'That's preposterous! With those hedgehoggy legs! Well, I'm perfectly willing if you have such an absurd fancy for it. What shall we wager?'

'A golden sovereign and a bottle of brandy.'

'Done. Shake paws on it. We might as well do it at once.'

But the hedgehog said, 'Nay, nay, there's no rush. I'm going home for some breakfast. I'll be back at this spot in half an hour.'

The hare was quite satisfied with this, so the hedgehog set off home. On his way he thought to himself, 'The hare is betting on his long legs, but I'll get the better of him. He may be an important gentleman, but he's a foolish fellow and he'll pay for what he's said.'

When the hedgehog got back home, he called to his wife, 'Wife, dress yourself quickly. You've got to come up to the field with me.'

'What's going on?' said his wife. 'I've made a wager with the hare for a gold sovereign and a bottle of brandy, and we have to race each other. You must be there.'

But his wife was aghast. 'Husband, are you not right in the head? Have you completely lost your marbles? What are you thinking of, running a race with the hare?'

The hedgehog snapped, 'Hold your tongue, woman, that's my affair. Don't try to discuss things which are matters for men. Now get yourself dressed and come with me.'

What else was the wife of a hedgehog to do? She had to obey him, like it or like it not.

So they set off together and the hedgehog told his wife, 'Pay attention to what I'm saying. The long field will be our racecourse. I'll run in one furrow and the hare in the other. We'll start from the top. You position yourself at the bottom of the furrow. When the hare arrives at the end of the furrow next to you, just shout out, "I'm here already."'

They reached the field. The hedgehog showed his wife her place, then walked up top to meet the hare.

'Shall we start then?' said the hare.

'Ready when you are,' said the hedgehog.

'Then both at once.'

They each got in their furrow. The hare counted, 'Once. Twice. Thrice and away!' and flew off at the speed of arrogance down the field. But the hedgehog only ran three steps, then crouched down, quiet and sleekit in his furrow.

As soon as the hare arrived full pelt at the bottom of the field, the hedgehog's wife was already there saying, 'I'm here already.' The hare was flabbergasted. He thought it really was the hedgehog because the wife looked just like her husband. But he thought, 'This hasn't been done fairly.' He said, 'We must run again. Let us do it now.' And a second time he whooshed off like a whirlwind. But the hedgehog's wife stayed prettily in her place and when the hare reached the other end of the field, there was the hedgehog himself crying out, 'I'm here already!' The hare was hopping with fury, and kept saying, 'Again! Again! We must run it again!' The hedgehog said, 'Fine. I'm happy to run as often as you choose.'

The hare ran another seventy-three times. Each time, the hedgehog tricked him. Every time the hare reached one end of the field, the hedgehog or his wife said, 'I'm here already.' But at the seventy-fourth time, the hare couldn't make it to the end. He collapsed in the middle of the field and a ribbon of blood streamed from his mouth. The hare was dead. The hedgehog ran up and took the gold sovereign, which he had won, and the bottle of brandy. He called his wife out of the furrow and the pair of them strolled home on their eight legs in great delight. If they're not dead, they're still living there.

The moral of this story is, firstly, that no matter how grand a person might be, they should not poke fun at anyone beneath themselves – not even a hedgehog. Secondly, it shows that a man should marry someone in his own position, who looks just like he looks himself. Whoever is a hedgehog must make quite sure that his wife is a hedgehog as well. And so on. And forth. Or fifth.

Travelling

poor woman had a son and the son longed to travel. But his mother said, 'How can you go travelling? We have no money for you to take with you.'

Then the son said, 'I will manage very well for myself. I will always say "Not much, not much".' So he walked for a long time and always said, 'Not much, not much, not much.' Then he passed by a group of fishermen and said, 'Good luck to you. Not much, not much, not much.'

And when the net was hauled in, they hadn't caught much fish. So one of them grabbed the youth and waved his stick and said, 'Do you want to feel the end of this?'

'What should I have said, then?' asked the youth.

'You must say "Lots more, lots more".'

After this, he walked on for a long time, saying, 'Lots more, lots more,' until he came to the gallows where they were about to hang a poor sinner. He called out, 'Good morning. Lots more, lots more.'

'What did you say, big mouth, lots more? Do you want to make out there are more wicked people to hang? Isn't this enough?' He got some more thwacks on his back.

'What should I have said?'

'You must say "God have mercy on the poor soul".'

So, once more, the lad walked for a long time saying, 'God have mercy on the poor soul.' He came to a pit where a knacker was chopping up a dead horse. The lad said, 'Good morning. God have mercy on the poor soul.'

'What did you say, you cheeky layabout?' The knacker gave him such a clout on the ear that he saw stars.

'What should I say, then?'

'You must say, "Into the pit it must go".'

He walked on again, saying, 'Into the pit it must go, into the pit it must go.' He came to a cart full of people. He said, 'Good morning, into the pit it must go.' Then the cart and everyone in it fell into a pit and the driver grabbed his whip and cracked it over the boy's back. He was forced to crawl home to his mother, and as long as he lived he never went travelling again. Never again, never again.

Snow White

n the cold heart of winter, when snow fell as though the white sky had been torn into a million pieces, a Queen sat by a window sewing. The frame of the window was made of black ebony. And while the Queen was sewing and looking out at the snow, she pricked her finger with the needle and three drops of blood fell upon the snow. The red looked so pretty against the white that the Queen suddenly thought to herself, 'I wish I had a child as white as snow, as red as blood and as black as the wood on the window-frame.'

Soon after that, she had a little daughter who was as white as snow, with lips as red as blood and hair as black as ebony. She was called Snow White and when she was born, the Queen died.

After a year had gone by, the King married again. His new wife was a beautiful woman, but she was proud and vain and couldn't bear the thought of anyone else being more beautiful. She owned a wonderful mirror and when she stood before it, looking at her reflection, and said:

'Mirror, mirror on the wall,
Who in this land is fairest of all?'

The mirror replied:

'You are, Queen. Fairest of all.'

Then she was pleased because she knew the mirror always told the truth.

But Snow White was growing up, and becoming more and more lovely. And when she was seven years old she was as beautiful as the day and ever, and more beautiful than the Queen herself. One day, the Queen asked her mirror:

'Mirror, mirror on the wall,
Who in this land is fairest of all?'

And the mirror answered:

'Queen, you are beautiful, day and night,
But even more stunning is little Snow White.'

Then the Queen got a shock, and turned yellow and green with poisonous envy. From that moment, whenever she looked at Snow White, her heart turned sour in her breast, she hated her so much. Jealousy and pride crept and coiled round her heart like ugly weeds, so that she could get no peace night or day. At last she called a huntsman and said, 'Take the girl into the forest. I want her out of my sight. Kill her – and fetch me back her lungs and liver to prove it.'

The huntsman did what she said and took Snow White away – but when he pulled out his knife to stab her innocent heart, Snow White cried and said, 'Please, dear huntsman, spare my life! I will run away into the wild woods and never come back.'

And as she was so beautiful, the huntsman took pity on her and said, 'Poor child. Run away then . . . The wild beasts will eat you soon enough,' he thought, but he felt as though a cruel hand had stopped squeezing his heart because he wasn't going to kill her. A young boar ran by and he slaughtered it, cut out its lungs and liver and took them to the Queen to prove the girl was dead. The cook had to salt them and the bad Queen ate them up and thought she'd eaten Snow White's lungs and liver.

But Snow White was alone in the forest and terrified. She began to run, over stones as sharp as malice, through thorns as spiteful as long fingernails. Wild beasts ran past her but did her no harm. She ran as long as her feet could carry her, until it was almost evening. It was then that she saw a little cottage and went into it to rest. Everything in the cottage was small, but neater and cleaner than can be described. There was a table with a white tablecloth and seven little plates, each with a little spoon. There were seven little knives and forks and seven little tankards. Against the wall were seven little beds side by side, each one covered with the whitest eiderdown.

Snow White was so hungry and thirsty that she ate a bite of bread and vegetables from each plate and sipped a swallow of wine from each mug. She was so sleepy that she lay down on one of the little beds, but none of them suited her. One was too long, one too short, one too soft, one too hard, one too lumpy, one too smooth. But the seventh was just right, so she snuggled down in it, said a prayer, and went to sleep.

When it was dark, the owners of the cottage came back. They were seven dwarfs who worked in the mountains digging for gold and copper. They lit their seven candles to fill the cottage with light and at once saw that someone had been there.

The first said: 'Who's been sitting in my chair?'

The second: 'Who's been eating off my plate?'

The third: 'Who's had some of my bread?'

The fourth: 'Who's been biting my vegetables?'

The fifth: 'Who's been using my fork?'

The sixth: 'Who's been cutting with my knife?'

Then the first one looked about and saw there was a little hollow on his bed, and he said, 'Who's been lying on my bed?' The others crowded round and each one shouted out, 'Somebody's been getting into my bed too!' But the seventh one found Snow White lying asleep in his bed, and he called the others. They cried out with amazement and fetched their seven little candles and let the light fall on Snow White. 'Oh goodness! Oh mercy!' they said. 'What a beautiful child.'

They were so pleased that they let her sleep peacefully on. The seventh dwarf slept with his companions, one hour with each, and so passed the night, and was glad to do so.

When morning came, Snow White awoke and was frightened when she saw the seven dwarfs. But they were friendly and asked her her name. 'My name is Snow White,' she replied. 'How have you come to our house?' asked the dwarfs. She told them that her stepmother had ordered her to be killed, but that the huntsman had taken pity on her and she had run through the forest for a whole day until she arrived at their little cottage.

The dwarf said, 'If you will take care of our house, make the beds, set the table, keep everything neat and tidy, cook, wash, sew, knit and mend, you can stay here with us and you shall want for nothing.'

'With all my heart!' said Snow White, and she stayed with the seven dwarfs. She kept the house exactly as they wanted. In the mornings they went off to the mountain to dig and delve for copper and gold. In the evenings they returned and then their supper had to be ready. The young girl was alone all day, so the dwarfs warned her to be careful. 'Beware of your stepmother. She will soon find out you are here. Don't let anyone into the house.'

But the Queen believed that she'd eaten the lungs Snow White breathed with, and that once again she was more beautiful than anyone. She went to her mirror and said:

'*Mirror, mirror, on the wall,*
Who in this land is fairest of all?'

And the mirror replied:

'*Queen, you're the fairest I can see.*
But deep in the wood where seven dwarfs dwell,
Snow White is still alive and well
And you are not so fair as she.'

Then the Queen was appalled because she knew that the mirror never lied and that the huntsman had tricked her. Her envious heart gnawed away inside her and her wicked mind thought and thought how she might kill Snow White – for so long as she wasn't the fairest in the land she could have no peace.

When at last she had thought of a plan, she stained

her face and dressed up like an old pedlar woman, so that not even her own mirror would have known her. In this disguise she made her way to the house of the seven dwarfs. She knocked at the door and sang out, 'Pretty things for sale, very cheap, very cheap.'

Snow White looked out of the window and called back, 'Good day, pedlar woman, what are you selling today?'

'Beautiful things, pretty things, fair things, skirt-laces of all colours.'

The sly Queen pulled out a lace of bright-coloured silk. 'I can let this friendly old woman in,' thought Snow White, and she unlocked the door and bought the fine laces.

But the old woman said, 'Child, what a sight you are! Come here and let the old pedlar woman lace you properly for once.' Snow White wasn't suspicious at all and stood before her and let herself be laced with the new laces. But the old woman laced so quickly and viciously and tightly that Snow White lost her breath and fell down as if she were dead. 'Now I am the most beautiful,' crowed the Queen and hurried away.

Soon afterwards, when evening fell, the seven

dwarfs came home – but how distressed they were to see their dear little Snow White lying on the ground. They lifted her up and, when they saw she was laced too tightly, they cut the laces. Then Snow White started to breathe a little and after a while came back to life. When the dwarfs heard what had happened, they said, 'The old pedlar woman was no one else but the evil Queen. Be careful. Let nobody in when we are not with you.'

The Queen ran home and went straight to her mirror:

'Mirror, mirror, on the wall.
Who in this land is fairest of all?'

And the mirror replied as before:

'Deep in the wood where seven dwarfs dwell,
Snow White is still alive and well.
Although you're the fairest I can see,
Queen, you are not so fair as she.'

When she heard the mirror's words, the Queen's blood flooded her heart with fear, for she knew it was true that Snow White was alive.

But she said, 'Now I will think of something that will really rid me of you for ever.' And by the help of witchcraft, which she understood, she made a poisonous comb. Then she disguised herself in the shape of another old woman, made her malevolent way to the house of the seven dwarfs and knocked at the door.

'Good things for sale, cheap, cheap.'

Snow White looked out and said, 'Go away, please. I can't let anyone in.

'You can at least look,' said the old woman, and held out the poisonous comb.

Snow White admired the comb so much that she let herself be fooled and opened the door. When they had agreed a price, the old woman said, 'Now I'll comb your ebony hair properly for once.'

Poor Snow White had no suspicion and let the old woman do as she wished. But no sooner had the crone put the comb in the girl's hair than the poison took effect and Snow White fell down senseless.

'You prize beauty,' spat the wicked woman. 'You are nothing now.' And she went away.

As luck would have it, it was nearly evening, when

the seven dwarfs were due home. When they saw Snow White left for dead on the ground they at once suspected the stepmother, and they looked and found the poisonous comb. They took it out and Snow White soon came to herself and told them what had happened. Then they warned her once more to be on her guard and to open the door to no one.

The Queen was at home with her mirror:

'Mirror, mirror, on the wall,
Who in this land is fairest of all?'

The mirror answered as before:

'Queen, you're the fairest I can see.
But deep in the woods where seven dwarfs dwell
Snow White is still alive and well
And no one's as beautiful as she.'

When she heard the mirror speak like this, the Queen trembled and shook with rage and swore, 'Snow White shall die, even if it costs me my life.'

She went into a quiet, secret, lonely room where no one ever came, and there she made a very poisonous apple. On the outside it looked pretty – crisp and white with a blood-red cheek, so that everyone who saw it longed for it – but whoever ate a piece of it would die.

Then she painted her face, disguised herself as a farmer's wife, and went for the third time to the house of the seven dwarfs. She knocked at the door. Snow White put her head out of the window and said, 'I can't let anyone in. The seven dwarfs have forbidden me.'

'It's all the same to me, dear. I'll soon get rid of my apples. Here – you can have one.'

'No, I dare not take anything.'

'Are you afraid it might be poisoned? Look, I'll cut the apple in two pieces, you eat the red cheek and I will eat the white.' But the apple was so cunningly made that only the red cheek was poisoned. Snow White longed for the tantalising fruit and when she saw the farmer's wife sink her teeth into it, she couldn't resist any more and stretched out her hand and took the poisonous half. But as soon as she'd taken a bite into her mouth, she fell down dead. The Queen gazed at her long and hard with a dreadful look and laughed horribly and said:

'*Snow White,*
Blood Red,
Black as Coffin Wood –
This time the seven dwarfs
Will find you dead for good.'

She went home quickly. She rushed to her mirror. She asked it again:

'*Mirror, mirror on the wall,*
Who in this land is fairest of all?'

And the mirror answered at last:

'*Oh, Queen, in this land you are fairest of all.*'

When the dwarfs came home in the evening, they found Snow White lying on the ground. She breathed no longer and was dead. They lifted her up and looked for anything poisonous, unlaced her, combed her hair, washed her in water and wine, but it was all useless. The girl was dead and stayed dead. So they laid her upon a bier and the seven of them sat round it and for three whole days they wept for Snow White.

Then they were going to bury her, but she still looked so alive with her pretty red cheeks. They said, 'We cannot put her in the cold, dark earth.' So they had a coffin of glass made, so that she could be seen from all sides. They laid her in it and put her name on it in gold letters and that she was daughter of a King. They placed the coffin up on the mountain and one of them always guarded it. Birds came, too, to weep for Snow White. First an owl, then a raven and last a dove.

And now Snow White lay for a very long time in her glass coffin as though she were only sleeping; still as white as snow, as red as blood, and with hair as black as ebony.

It happened, though, that a King's son came to the forest and went to the dwarfs' house to spend the night. He saw the coffin glinting like a mirror on the mountain, and he saw Snow White inside it and read what was written there in letters of gold. He said to the dwarfs, 'Let me have the coffin. I will give you anything you name for it.' But the dwarfs answered that they wouldn't part with it for all the treasure in the world. Then he said, 'Let me have it as a gift. My heart cannot beat without seeing Snow White. I will honour and cherish her above all else in this world.' Because he spoke like this, the dwarfs pitied him and gave him the coffin.

The King's son had it carried away on his servants' shoulders. As they did this, they tripped over some tree roots, and with the jolt the piece of poisonous apple which Snow White had swallowed came out of her throat. Before long, she opened her eyes, lifted the coffin lid and sat up, as warm and alive as love. 'Heavens, where am I?' she asked.

The King's son was shining like an apple with delight and said, 'You are with me.' He told her what had happened and said, 'I love you more than my heart can hold. Come with me to my father's palace. Be my wife.'

Snow White was willing and did go with him, and their wedding was held with great show and splendour. Snow White's wicked stepmother was summoned to the feast. When she was dressed in her best jewels and finery, she danced to her mirror and queried:

'Mirror, mirror, on the wall,
Who in this land is fairest of all?'

The mirror answered:

'You are the old Queen. That much is true.
But the new young Queen is fairer than you.'

Then the wicked woman cursed and swore and was so demented, so wretched, so distraught, that she could hardly think. At first, she wouldn't go to the feast, but she had no peace, and had to see the young Queen. So she went. And when she walked in she

saw that it was Snow White and was unable to move
with fear and rage. She stood like a statue of hate.
But iron dancing shoes were already heating in the
fire. They were brought in with tongs and set before
her. Then she was forced to put on the red-hot shoes
and she was made to dance, dance, until she dropped
down dead.

The Ungrateful Son

nce upon a time, a man and his wife were sat by their front door and they had before them a roasted chicken, which they were about to eat together. Just then, the man saw his old father coming and he quickly snatched up the chicken and hid it. The old man came, was given a drink of water, then sent away. As soon as he was gone, the son ran to fetch the chicken for the table. But when he picked it up, it had turned into a great toad, which jumped into his face and squatted there and never went away. If anyone tried to take it off, it spat poisonously and looked as though it would spring in their face – so in the end no one dared to touch it. The ungrateful son was forced to feed the toad every single day or else it fed itself on his face. And so he trudged from north to south and east to west and found no rest on any road and on his wretched face a toad.

The Wise Servant

ow lucky the master is, and how smoothly everything runs in his house, when he has a wise servant who listens to his orders carefully but doesn't carry them out, choosing instead to trust to his own ideas. Clever Hans was a type like this and was once sent out by his master to find a lost cow. He was gone for a very long time, and the master thought, 'Good old Hans doesn't do things by halves.' But when he didn't come back at all, the master was worried that something bad might have happened to Hans. He set out himself to look for him.

He had to look for ages, but at last he caught sight of the lad running up and down a large field. 'There you are, Hans,' he said when he caught up with him.

'Have you found the cow which I sent you to fetch?'

Hans answered, 'No, master, I've not found the cow. But I've not bothered looking for it either.'

'Then what have you been looking for, Hans?'

'Something much better, and I've found it too!'

'What is that, Hans?'

'Three blackbirds,' answered Hans.

'And where are they?'

'I can see one of them, I can hear the other, and I'm running after the third,' said Wise Hans.

Let this be a lesson for you. Don't bother yourself with your bosses or their orders. Just do whatever pops into your head, whenever you please, and then you'll be acting just as wisely as Clever Hans. Agreed?

The Musicians of Bremen

A man had a donkey who had worked hard for years carrying heavy sacks of corn to the mill. But the donkey's strength had gone and he was getting more and more unfit for the job. The man was thinking how he could get shut of him and save the expense of feeding him. But the donkey got wind of this and ran away. He set off towards Bremen and thought he might try his luck at being a town musician. After a while on the road, he came across a hound lying by the roadside, panting away as though he'd run very hard. So the donkey said, 'Hello, old Hound-Dog, what are you gasping like that for?'

The dog answered him, 'Och, I'm not getting any

younger and get weaker every day so I can't hunt any more. My master was going to kill me, so I ran away. But how shall I make my living now?' The donkey said, 'I'll tell you what. I'm on my way to Bremen to become a town musician. Why don't you come with me? I'll play the lute and you can bang away at the kettle-drum!'

The hound was chuffed with this idea and on they went.

Before long, they found a cat slumped by the roadside with a face like three wet Wednesdays.

'Now then, old Lick-Whiskers, what makes you look so miserable?'

The cat answered him, 'How else should I look with my problems? Just because I'm getting on and my teeth are worn to stumps and I prefer to sit dreaming by the fire rather than run about after mice, my mistress wants to drown me. So I've run away. But now, who's to tell me what to do and where to go?'

'Come with us to Bremen to be a town musician. You're well known for your caterwauling music of the night!'

The cat was impressed with this plan and on the

three of them went.

Quite soon our three runaways came to a farm and there on the gate perched a cockerel crowing like mad. The donkey called out, 'That terrible crowing's going right through us. What on earth's up?'

The cock explained, 'I'm forecasting fine weather, because today's washday in Heaven and Our Lady wants to dry Baby Jesus's tiny shirts. But they've got guests coming here for dinner tomorrow, and that callous, hard-hearted housekeeper has told cook to cook me. I've to have my head chopped off tonight, so I'm having a good crow while l can.'

'Outrageous, Redcomb! Come instead with us to Bremen. You'll be better off there than in a casserole. With that voice of yours and our rhythm, we're going to make music the like of which has never been heard!'

The cock thought this seemed an excellent plan and all four of them went on their way together.

Bremen town was too far to reach in a day, though, and in the evening they came to a forest where they decided to spend the night. The donkey and the dog lay down under a large tree, the cat settled herself in the branches, and the cock flew right to the top and perched there. Before he went to sleep, he looked north, south, east and west and thought he spied a quaver of light in the distance. So he called down to his fellow musicians that there must be a house nearby for him to see a light. The donkey said, 'Then let's go and find it. The accommodation here's appalling.' The hound said that he wouldn't turn up his nose at a plate of bones with some meat on them.

So they set off in the direction of the light, which got bigger and brighter and more attractive, until they came to a well-lit house, where a band of robbers lived. The donkey, who was the biggest, sneaked up to the window and peeped in.

'What can you see, old Greymule?' asked the cock.

'What can I see! Only a table groaning with wonderful things to eat and drink and a band of robbers sat round it filling their boots!'

'Those words are music to my ears! That's the kind of thing we're after,' said the cock.

'Yes, yes! If only we were inside!'

So the four famished fugitives put their furry or feathery heads together to decide how to get rid of the robbers. At last they thought of a plan. Old Greymule was to stand on his hind legs with his forefeet on the window; Old Hound-Dog was to jump on the donkey's back; Old Lick-Whiskers was to climb on the back of the dog; and lastly Redcomb was to fly up and perch on the head of the cat, like a hat.

When they'd finally managed all this, the donkey gave a signal, and they launched into their music. The donkey bray-hay-hayed. The cat made mew-mew-music. The hound went wopbopawoofwoofbowwowwow. And the cock gave a great big doody-doodle-doo. For an encore, they all crashed into the room through the window, smashing the glass and still singing. At this horrifying din, the robbers jumped up and thought that a banshee had come screaming into the house. The robbers were so terrified for their lives that they fled, freaked, into the forest. At this our four friends sat down at the table, well pleased with what was left, and feasted as though they wouldn't see food and drink for a fortnight.

When our four musicians had finished their meal, they put out the light and found somewhere comfortable to sleep, each according to his needs and nature. The donkey dossed down in the dung heap in the yard. The hound hunched down behind

the door. The cat curled up near the ashes on the hearth. And the cock flapped up to roost in the rafters. They were all so tired after their long journey that they soon fell fast asleep.

The robbers were watching the house from a safe distance. When midnight had passed, and they saw that the light was out and all was quiet, their captain said, 'Well, now. Perhaps we shouldn't have let ourselves be frightened off so easily.' He ordered one of his men to go back to the house and investigate.

The man found everything as silent and dark as a closed piano lid, as hushed as drowned bagpipes. He fetched a candle from the kitchen. He thought that the burning red eyes of the cat were glowing coals and stuck his match in them to light it. But the cat didn't appreciate the humour of this and flew in his face, scratching and spitting. The man was terrified out of his wits and ran for the back door – but he trod on the dog who leaped up and bit him savagely on the leg. He fled for his life into the yard and was about to leap over the dung heap when he received a whopping kick in the arse from the donkey. All this commotion had wakened the cock, who began to crow on his perch. 'Cock-a-doodle-doo! Cock-a-doodle-doo!'

The robber ran as fast as he could back to his mates and said to the captain, 'Oh my God! There's a horrible witch in the house. I felt her ratty breath and her long claws on my face. Oh God! There's a man with a knife by the back door who stabbed me in the leg. Oh! There's a black monster in the yard who beat me with a wooden club. God! And to top it all, there's a judge on the roof and he called out, "That's the crook that'll do! The crook that'll do!" So I got out of there as fast as I could.'

After that, the robbers didn't dare go back to the house. But the four talented members of the Bremen Town Band liked the house so much that they just stayed on. And they're still there.

This story has been told for yonks. The mouth of the last person to tell this tale still has a warm tongue in it – as you can see.

The Golden Key

It was winter, and deep snow covered the ground, when a poor boy was made to go out on a sledge to fetch wood. When he had gathered enough, and packed it all, he thought that before he went home he would light a fire to warm his frozen limbs. So he scraped away the snow and as he was making a clear space he found a tiny golden key. As soon as he picked it up he thought that where there was a key there must also be a lock. So he dug in the ground and discovered a small iron chest. He thought, 'If the key only fits there are bound to be precious treasures in this little box.' He searched everywhere but couldn't find a keyhole. At last he found one which was so small

that it could hardly be seen. He tried the key in the lock and it fitted perfectly. Then he turned the key round once. And now we must wait until he has quite finished unlocking it and then we shall find out what wonderful things were hidden in that box . . .

Rumpelstiltskin

here was a miller once who was very poor but he had one daughter more beautiful than any treasure. It happened one day that he came to speak to the King and to make himself look special he said, 'I have a daughter who can spin straw into gold.' Now this King was very fond of gold, so he said to the miller, 'That's a talent that would please me hugely. If your daughter is as clever as you say, bring her to my palace tomorrow and I'll put her to the test.'

When the girl was brought to him, he led her to a room that was full of straw, gave her a spinning-wheel and said, 'Set to work. You have all night ahead of you. But if you haven't spun all this straw into gold by dawn, you must die.' Then he locked the door with his own hands and left her there alone.

The poor miller's daughter sat there without a clue what to do. She had no idea how to spin straw into gold and she grew more and more frightened and started to cry.

Suddenly the door opened and in came a little man who said, 'Good evening, Mistress Miller, why are you crying?'

'Oh, I have to spin this straw into gold and I don't know how to do it.'

'What will you give me if I do it for you?'

'My necklace.'

'Done.'

The little man took the necklace, squatted down before the spinning-wheel, and whirr, whirr, whirr! Three turns and the bobbin was full. And so he went on all night and at sunrise all the bobbins were full of gold.

First thing in the morning, in came the King and when he saw all the gold he was amazed and delighted. But the gold-greed grew in his heart and he had the miller's daughter taken to an even bigger room filled up with straw and told her to spin the lot into gold if she valued her life. She really didn't know

what to do and was crying when the door opened. In stepped the little man again saying, 'What will you give me if I spin all this straw into gold?'

'The ring from my finger.'

So the little man took the ring and whirred away at the wheel all the long dark night and by dawn each dull strand of straw was glistening gold. The King was beside himself with pleasure at the treasure, but his desire for gold still wasn't satisfied. He took the miller's daughter to an even larger room full of straw and told her, 'You must spin all of this into gold tonight and if you succeed you shall be my wife.' And the King said to himself, 'She might only be the daughter of a miller, but I won't find a richer woman anywhere.'

As soon as the girl was alone, the little man appeared for the third time and said, 'What will you give me this time if I spin the straw into gold for you?'

'I have nothing left to give.'

'Then you must promise to give me the first child you have after you are Queen.'

'Who knows what the future holds,' thought the girl. And as she had no choice, she gave her word to the little man. At once he started to spin until all the straw was gold.

When the King arrived in the morning and saw everything just as he wished, he held the wedding at once and the miller's beautiful daughter became a Queen.

After a year she brought a gorgeous golden child into the world and thought no more of the little man. But one day he stepped suddenly into her room and said, 'Now give me what you promised.'

The Queen was truly horrified and offered him all the gold and riches of the kingdom if he would only leave the child. But the little man said, 'No, I'd rather have a living child than all the treasure in the world.' At this, the Queen began to sob so bitterly that the little man took pity on her and said, 'I'll give you three days. If you can find out my name by then, you can keep your child.'

The Queen sat up all night, searching her brains for his name like someone sieving for gold. She went through every single name she could think of. She sent out a messenger to ask everywhere in the land for all the names that could be found. On the next day, when the little man came, she recited the whole alphabet of names that she'd learnt, starting with Balthasar, Casper, Melchior . . . But to each one the little man said, 'That isn't my name.'

On the second day, she sent servants all round the neighbourhood to find more names and she tried all the strange and unusual ones on the little man. 'Perhaps you're called Shortribs or Sheepshanks or Lacelegs.' But he always said, 'That isn't my name.' On the third day, the messenger came back and said, 'I haven't managed to find a single new name, but as I approached a high mountain at the end of the forest, the place where fox and hare bid each other goodnight, I saw a small hut. There was a fire burning outside it and round the fire danced an absurd little man. He hopped on one leg and bawled:

'Bake today! Tomorrow brew!

Then I'll take the young Queen's child!

She will cry and wish she knew

That RUMPELSTILTSKIN's how I'm styled!'

You may imagine how overjoyed the Queen was when she heard the name. And when soon afterwards the little man stalked in and demanded, 'Well, Mistress Queen, what is my name?', she started by saying, 'Is it Jacob?' 'No.' 'Is it Wilhelm?' 'No.' 'Is it Grimm?' 'No.' 'Perhaps your name is Rumpelstiltskin?' 'The devil has told you! The devil has told you!' shrieked the little man. In his fury he stamped his right foot so hard on the ground that it went right in up to his waist. And then in a rage he pulled at his left leg so hard with the very same hands that had spun the straw into gold – that he tore himself in two. Tore. Himself. In. Two.

Fair Katrinelje

ood day, Father Hollowtree.' 'Thank you, Pif Paf Poltrie.' 'May I marry your daughter?' 'Oh yes, if Mother Milkmoo, Brother Proudclogs, Sister Makecheese and the fair Katrinelje are willing, you can marry her.'

'Then where is Mother Milkmoo?'
'She's in the barn a-milking the coo.'

'Good day, Mother Milkmoo.' 'Thank you, Pif Paf Poltrie.' 'May I marry your daughter?' 'Oh yes, if Father Hollowtree, Brother Proudclogs, Sister Makecheese and the fair Katrinelje are willing, you can marry her.'

'Then where is Brother Proudclogs?'
'He's in the woodshed, a-chopping logs.'

'Good day, Brother Proudclogs.' 'Thank you, Pif Paf Poltrie.' 'May I marry your sister?' 'Oh yes, if Father Hollowtree, Mother Milkmoo, Sister Makecheese and the fair Katrinelje are willing, you can marry her.'

'Then where is Sister Makecheese?'
'She's in the kitchen a-shelling peas.'

'Good day, Sister Makecheese.' 'Thank you, Pif Paf Poltrie.' 'May I marry your sister?' 'Oh yes, if Father Hollowtree, Mother Milkmoo, Brother Proudclogs and the fair Katrinelje are willing, you can marry her.'

'Then where is the fair Katrinelje?'
'She's a-counting her pennies in the parlour.'

'Good day, fair Katrinelje.' 'Thank you, Pif Paf Poltrie.' 'Will you marry me?' 'Oh yes, if Father Hollowtree, Mother Milkmoo, Brother Proudclogs and Sister Make-cheese are willing, then you can have me.'

'Fair Katrinelje, how much dowry do you have?'

'Fourteen pennies in hard cash, two-and-a-half pennies owing to me, half a pound of dried fruits, a quarter of roots and two ounces of shoots.

'All these things and more are mine.
'Don't you think my dowry's fine?'

'Pif Paf Poltrie, what is your trade? Are you a tailor?'

'Even better.'

'A cobbler?'

'Even better.'

'A ploughman?'

'Even better.'

'A joiner?'

'Even better.'

'A blacksmith?'

'Even better'

'A miller?'

'Even better.

'Perhaps you're a broom-maker.'

'Yes! So I am! You clever maid. And isn't that a useful trade?'

Brother Scamp

nce there was a great war and when it was over many soldiers were discharged. One of these was Brother Scamp. He was given one loaf of ammunition-bread and four shillings and sent on his way. St Peter, however, had disguised himself as a beggarman and was sitting by the roadside. When Brother Scamp came along, he begged for charity. Brother Scamp answered him, 'Dear beggarman, what am I to give you? I have been a soldier, but on my dismissal I was given only this loaf of ammunition-bread and four shillings. Once they've gone, I shall have to beg myself. Even so, I'll give you something.' Then Brother Scamp divided his loaf into four parts, gave one to St Peter, and gave him a shilling as well.

The apostle thanked him and hurried on his way; but further along the road he sat down again disguised as a different beggar. When Brother Scamp came along, he begged for a gift as before. Brother Scamp spoke as he had earlier and again gave him a piece of bread and a shilling. St Peter thanked him and went on, but for the third time sat down in Brother Scamp's path disguised as a beggar. He begged again. Brother Scamp spoke as before and again gave him a quarter of bread and a shilling. St Peter thanked him.

Brother Scamp, with only one shilling and the last morsel of bread left, went on to an inn, where he ate the bread and ordered a shilling's worth of ale. When he had finished, he set off once more and soon met St Peter, this time dressed up as a discharged soldier like himself.

'Good day, comrade. Can you spare a bit of bread and a shilling for some beer?'

'Where would I find them?' said Brother Scamp. 'I've been discharged and all the army gave me was a loaf of ammunition-bread and four shillings. I met three beggars on the road and I gave each of them a quarter of bread and a shilling. I ate the last quarter of bread at an inn and spent the last shilling on ale. So now my pockets are empty. If you're in the same boat, then let us go begging together.'

St Peter said, 'There's no need to do that. I know a bit about healing. I'll soon earn as much as I need from that.'

'Well,' said Brother Scamp, 'I know nothing at all about that, so I'd better go begging on my own.'

'Just come along with me,' said St Peter, 'and if I make any money at it you can have half.'

'Fair play,' said Brother Scamp, and the two soldiers went on their way together.

They soon came to a peasant's house, inside which they heard loud sobbing and cries of lamentation. They went in. A man lay there, very sick and at death's door, and his poor wife was bawling her lungs out. 'Stop your weeping and wailing,' said St Peter. 'I will make this man well again.' He took some ointment from his pocket and healed the man quicker than an angel's wing. The man stood up in the best of health.

The husband and wife were overjoyed and said, 'How can we thank you? What can we give you to repay you?' But St Peter wouldn't accept any reward; and the more the peasant folk offered, the more he refused. Brother Scamp nudged St Peter. 'Take something, for God's sake. We need it!' Finally, the woman brought in a lamb and told St Peter that he really must take it. But St Peter didn't want to. Then Brother Scamp gave him a poke and said, 'Take it, take it. We need it.' At last St Peter said, 'All right, I'll accept it. But I won't carry it. If you want it so much, then you can carry it.' 'Fair play,' said Brother Scamp, and hoisted the lamb onto his shoulder.

They journeyed on together and came to a forest. By now, Brother Scamp was beginning to find the lamb very heavy, and he was famished as well. So he said to his companion, 'Look, this is a good spot. Let's stop and cook the lamb and eat it.' 'If you like,' said St Peter, 'but I don't know anything about cooking. If you want to cook, there's a pot. I shall go for a walk until it's ready. But you mustn't start eating until I return. I will come back at the right time.' 'Off you pop,' said Brother Scamp, 'I'm a nifty hand at cooking. Just leave everything to me.'

When St Peter had gone, Brother Scamp butchered the lamb, lit the fire, threw the meat into the pot and cooked it. After a while, the meat was ready, but St Peter still hadn't returned. Brother Scamp removed the meat from the pot, cut it up, and found the heart. 'That's supposed to be the best part,' he thought to himself. He tasted a little bit, then a little bit more, and a little bit more, and soon he had eaten it all up. Eventually, St Peter came back and said, 'You can eat the whole lamb yourself. Just give me the heart.'

Brother Scamp took a knife and fork and pretended to look for the heart. He poked and prodded anxiously among the flesh and finally gave up. 'There isn't any heart,' he said.

'How is that possible?' said St Peter.

'Search me,' said Brother Scamp. 'But hang on a minute! What fools we are! Everyone knows that a lamb hasn't got a heart.' 'Let's go then. If there's no heart, I don't want any lamb. You can have it all for yourself.'

'What I can't eat now, I'll take away in my knapsack,' said Brother Scamp. He ate up half the lamb and packed the rest into his knapsack.

They went on their way and after a while St Peter arranged for a great stream of water to block their path. They had to get across it and St Peter said, 'You go first.' But Brother Scamp said, 'No, you go first, comrade.' And he thought, 'If the water proves too deep for him, I can stay behind.'

St Peter waded across and the water only came up to his knees. So Brother Scamp followed him, but the water got deeper and deeper until it was up to his neck. Then he cried out, 'Brother! Help me!'

'Confess you ate the lamb's heart!'

'No! I didn't eat it!'

The water grew even deeper until it was up to his mouth. Brother Scamp cried out again, 'Brother! Help me!'

'Admit you ate the lamb's heart!'

'No! I didn't eat it!'

But St Peter would not let the man drown, so he made the water go down and helped him across.

They took to the road again and came to a kingdom where they heard that the King's daughter was ill and on the verge of death. The soldier turned to St Peter. 'Now then, Brother! This looks like just the thing for us. If we can cure her, we'll be sorted for life!' St Peter agreed, but walked too slowly for Brother Scamp's liking. 'Come on, Brother, hurry up. We want to get there before it's too late.' But the more Brother Scamp pushed and prodded, the slower St Peter went; and before long they heard that the Princess had died.

'I knew it!' said Brother Scamp. 'This is what comes of your dawdling along.'

'Hold your tongue,' said St Peter. 'I don't just heal sick people. I can make dead people live again.'

'Well, if that's the case,' said Brother Scamp, 'make sure we get a decent reward. Ask for half the kingdom at least.'

They went to the royal palace where everyone was distraught with grief. St Peter went straight to the King and vowed to him that he would bring his daughter back to life. He was taken to her room and said, 'Bring me a cauldron of water.'

They brought the water and he told everyone to leave the room except for Brother Scamp. St Peter cut off the dead girl's limbs and tossed them into the water. He made a fire under the cauldron and boiled them. When all the flesh had fallen off, he took the clean white bones out of the water, placed them on a table, and arranged them in the correct order. When he'd done all this to his satisfaction, he stepped forward and said three times, 'In the name of the Holy Trinity, dead Princess, stand up and live again.'

At the third time, the girl stood up, warm and healthy and beautiful. The King was shaking with joy and gratitude and said to St Peter, 'Name your reward. Even if you ask for half my kingdom you shall have it.' But St Peter replied, 'I want nothing.'

'Oh, you cabbage-head!' thought Brother Scamp. He jabbed his comrade in the ribs and said, 'Don't be so stupid. You might not want a reward, but I do.' St Peter still wanted nothing, but the King saw that the other man felt quite the opposite and ordered his treasurer to fill Brother Scamp's knapsack with gold.

Again they went on their way. When they came to a forest, St Peter said to Brother Scamp, 'Now we'll share out the gold.' 'Fair play.' St Peter divided the gold into three parts. Brother Scamp thought to himself, 'What nonsense has he got into his head now? Why divide the gold into three when there's only two of us?'

St Peter spoke. 'I've split the gold perfectly. One part for me, one for you, and one for whoever ate the lamb's heart.' 'That was me!' said Brother Scamp, and scooped up the gold as fast as a double-wink. 'I give you my word.'

'How is that possible,' said St Peter, 'when we know that a lamb has no heart?'

'What are you on about, Brother? Everyone knows

a lamb has a heart just like any other animal. Why on earth shouldn't it?'

'Very well,' said St Peter, 'keep the gold for yourself. I have had enough of your company and I'm going on by myself.'

'If that's what you want then fair play, Brother,' the soldier said. 'Goodbye.'

So St Peter took a different road and Brother Scamp thought, 'I'm glad to see the back of him. What a strange individual he turned out to be.' He now had plenty of money, but he didn't know how to use it sensibly. He squandered some, gave some away, and after a while he was penniless once more. He came to a land where he was told that the King's daughter had died. He thought to himself, 'Hang about! There might be something in this for me. I'll bring her back to life and make sure I get a decent reward.' So he went straight to the King and offered to return his daughter from the dead. The King had heard that there was a discharged soldier going around bringing the dead back to life. He thought that Brother Scamp might be this man, but he wasn't certain. So he asked the advice of his counsellor, who said that, since his daughter was dead, he had nothing to lose.

Brother Scamp requested a cauldron of water and ordered everyone from the room. Then he severed the dead girl's limbs, tossed them into the water, lit a fire, exactly as he had seen St Peter do. The water bubbled up. When the flesh fell away from the bones, he took them out and laid them on the table; but he had no idea of the correct order and got the beautiful white bones all jumbled up. Nevertheless, he stepped up to the table and cried, 'In the name of the Holy Trinity, rise from the dead.' He said it three times but not a bone budged. He said it three times more, but it was useless, and he shouted, 'Blasted girl! Get up off that table or I'll half-kill you!'

The words had no sooner left his mouth than St Peter came in through the window, once again disguised as a discharged soldier.

'Blasphemous, godless man!' he said. 'What are you doing? How can the poor girl rise again when you've got her bones in such a mess!' 'I've done the best I could, Brother,' said Brother Scamp. 'I'll help you out just this once,' said St Peter, 'but if you ever try anything like this again, Heaven help you. Furthermore, you are neither to demand nor accept any reward at all from the King.'

Then St Peter arranged the bones in the right order and said three times, 'In the name of the Holy Trinity, rise from the dead.' The King's daughter breathed and arose, as healthy and beautiful as she ever was, and St Peter went out through the window. Brother Scamp was pleased things had worked out so well, but gutted at not being allowed to ask for his reward.

'That bloke's not the full shilling,' he thought. 'What he gives with one hand he takes away with the other. It's weird!'

The King offered Brother Scamp any reward he wanted. He refused, as he'd been ordered to, but with hints, winks, nudges, shuffles and shrugs, he got the King to fill his knapsack with gold and off he went.

St Peter was waiting at the palace gate. 'Just look at you! Didn't I forbid you to accept anything? And yet out you march as bold as brass with your knapsack bulging with gold.'

'I can't help it if they forced it on me,' said Brother Scamp.

'You'd better not try this sort of thing again or you'll wish you hadn't.'

'Have no fear on that score, Brother. Why should I bother to boil bones when I'm loaded with gold?'

'I can imagine how long your gold will last you,' said St Peter. 'But to keep you from meddling in forbidden ways again, I'll grant you the power to wish anything you please into your knapsack. Now goodbye to you. You will not see me again.'

'Goodbye,' said Brother Scamp and thought, 'Good riddance more like, you peculiar person. I shan't be running to catch up with you!' And he gave no more thought to the magical power of his knapsack.

Brother Scamp travelled on with his gold, and squandered and wasted it the same as before. When he only had four shillings left, he came to an inn. 'I might as well spend them,' he thought, and ordered up three shillings' worth of wine and one of bread. He sat drinking and the smell of roast goose filled his nostrils. When he looked around he saw two geese that the innkeeper was cooking in the oven. Suddenly he remembered that his companion had told him he could wish anything he pleased into his knapsack. 'Get in!' he thought. 'Let's see if it works with the geese.' He went outside and said, 'I wish those two geese were out of the oven and in my knapsack!' After saying the words, he unbuckled the knapsack, looked in, and there they were.

'This couldn't be better!' he said. 'I'm a made man!'

He sat down in a meadow and took out the geese. As he was busily eating, two journeymen came along and looked hungrily at the goose that hadn't been touched yet. Brother Scamp thought to himself, 'One goose is plenty for me,' and called over the two journeymen. 'Here, take this goose and wish me well as you eat it.' They thanked him, went into the inn, ordered a flask of wine and a loaf of bread, took out Brother Scamp's goose and began to eat. The innkeeper's wife had been watching them and said to her husband, 'That pair over there are eating a goose. Go and check it's not one of ours out of the oven.'

He went and looked and the oven was worse than gooseless. 'Hoy, you thieves! You think you're getting that goose pretty cheap, don't you? Pay up at once or I'll stripe your skins with a stick.' 'We're not thieves,' they protested. 'A discharged soldier gave us the goose out there in the meadow.'

'Don't try and pull the wool over my eyes,' said the innkeeper. 'There was a soldier here but he went out the door empty-handed. I saw him myself. You're the thieves and you'd better pay up.' But they couldn't pay, so he seized his stick and swiped them out of the inn.

Brother Scamp continued on his way and came to a place where there was a magnificent castle, and not far from it a miserable inn. He went to the inn and asked for a bed for the night, but the innkeeper refused him, saying, 'There is no room. The house is full of noblemen.' Brother Scamp said, 'That's odd. Why would they choose this place instead of that splendid castle?' 'Well, you see,' said the innkeeper, 'it's not easy to spend a night in that castle. Some have tried, but no one has ever come out alive.'

'If others have tried, so will I,' said Brother Scamp.

'Don't even think of it,' said mine host. 'It will be the end of you.'

But Brother Scamp insisted. 'Don't worry about me. Just give me the keys and something to eat and drink.'

So the man gave him the keys and some food and wine and Brother Scamp went into the castle and enjoyed his meal. After a while, he felt sleepy and lay down on the floor because there was no bed. He soon fell fast asleep, but in the middle of the night he was awakened by a terrifying noise. When he opened his

eyes, he saw nine ugly devils dancing round him in a circle. 'Dance as much as you like,' said Brother Scamp, 'but stay away from me.' The devils came closer and closer and nearly stepped on his face with their hideous feet.

'Stop it, you fiends!' he cried, but their frenzy got worse. Brother Scamp became very angry and shouted, 'Quiet, I said!' He grabbed a table leg and set about them with it, but nine devils were too many for one soldier. While he was hitting the one in front of him, the ones behind him grabbed his hair and yanked fiercely. 'Stinking devils! This is too much. But now I'll show you something. All nine of you, into my knapsack!' Wheesh! In they all went. He buckled the knapsack, flung it into a corner, and at last everything was still. Brother Scamp lay down again and slept until morning. The innkeeper and the nobleman who owned the castle arrived to see what had happened to him. They were astonished to find him alive and well and asked, 'Didn't the ghosts harm you?'

'How could they harm me? I've got them all in my knapsack. Now you can live in your castle again. The ghosts won't bother you any more.'

The nobleman thanked him, rewarded him generously and begged him to stay in his service and he would provide for him till death. But Brother Scamp said, 'No, I'm used to wandering about. I'll just get on my way.'

Back on the road, Brother Scamp stopped at a smithy, put the knapsack full of devils on the anvil, and asked the blacksmith and his apprentices to batter it with all their might. The devils screamed dreadfully, and when he opened the knapsack eight were dead, but one, who had been in a crease, was still alive. That one scuttled away and went to Hell.

After this, Brother Scamp travelled about for a long time, and if anyone knows what he got up to, they'll have a long tale to tell. Finally, he grew old and his thoughts turned to death; so he went to a hermit who was respected as a holy man and said, 'I'm tired of knocking about, and now I want to see about getting into the Kingdom of Heaven.' The hermit replied, 'There are two roads. One is broad and pleasant and leads to Hell. The other is narrow and rough and leads to Heaven.' Brother Scamp thought, 'I'd be daft to take the rough and narrow way.' Sure enough, he took the broad, pleasant way and fetched up at a big black gate.

It was the Gate of Hell. He knocked, and the gatekeeper squinted out to see who was there. When he saw Brother Scamp, he nearly leapt out of his skin, for he just happened to be the ninth devil in the knapsack who'd escaped with only a black eye. Fast as a rat, he slammed, locked and bolted the gate, and fled to the Head Devil.

'There's a man outside with a knapsack,' he said. 'He wants to come in, but for Hell's sake don't let him, or he'll wish all Hell into his knapsack. He had me in it once, and what a terrible battering I got!'

Brother Scamp was told he couldn't come in and should clear off. 'If they won't give me a welcome here,' he thought, 'I'll see if there's room for me in Heaven. I've got to stay somewhere.'

So he turned around and travelled until he came to the Gate of Heaven, and knocked upon it. St Peter happened to be on duty as gatekeeper, and Brother Scamp recognised him right away. 'Well, look who it is!' he thought. 'My old comrade will give me a warmer reception.'

But St Peter said, 'I don't believe it! You think you can get into Heaven?'

'Let me in, Brother, I've got to go somewhere. They wouldn't take me in Hell, or I wouldn't be stood here now.'

'Too bad,' said Peter. 'You're not getting in here.'

'Well,' said Brother Scamp, 'if you really won't allow me in then take back your knapsack, because I don't want to keep anything of yours.'

'Hand it over then,' said St Peter.

He passed the knapsack through the railings and St Peter hung it up behind his chair.

'Now,' said Brother Scamp, 'I wish myself into the knapsack.'

Whoosh! There he was in the knapsack, the knapsack was in Heaven, and St Peter had to let him stay there, fair play.

More Gems from
CAROL ANN DUFFY

'In the world of British poetry, Carol Ann Duffy is a superstar.' *Guardian*

In this delightful collection of poetry for children, Carol Ann Duffy takes us on a mud-and-all ramble through sand, socks, songs and schoolrooms.

A beautiful edition of this complete collection of the former Poet Laureate's poetry for children.

→ THE FABER CLASSICS LIBRARY ←

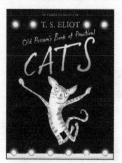

⤞ THE FABER CLASSICS LIBRARY ⤝

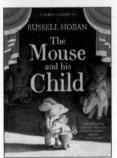

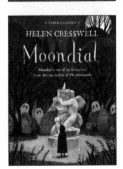

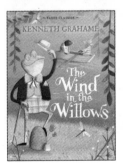